"To many offlanders, what you have here would be more precious than gold-pressed latinum."

Picard gazed at them with a mixture of envy and dread. "I'm afraid it's the reason ⋯⋯ trying to take this world away f⋯⋯

Artim gulped.

"If not for Data, you⋯⋯ ⋯⋯en relocated by now," the captain ⋯⋯ued. *And no one would ever know . . .*

"How can we possibly defend ourselves?" asked Tournel with concern.

"The moment we pick up a weapon," warned Sojef, "we become one of *them*. We lose everything we are—"

"It may not come to that. Clearly, the architects of this conspiracy have tried to keep it a secret. Not just from you, but from my people as well." Picard balled his hand into a fist. "I don't intend to let them."

Star Trek: The Next Generation
STARFLEET ACADEMY

1 Worf's First Adventure
2 Line of Fire
3 Survival
4 Capture the Flag
5 Atlantis Station
6 Mystery of the Missing Crew
7 Secret of the Lizard People
8 Starfall
9 Nova Command
#10 Loyalties
#11 Crossfire
#12 Breakaway
#13 The Haunted Starship
#14 Deceptions

Star Trek:
STARFLEET ACADEMY

#1 Crisis on Vulcan
#2 Aftershock
#3 Cadet Kirk

Star Trek: Deep Space Nine

1 The Star Ghost
2 Stowaways
3 Prisoners of Peace
4 The Pet
5 Arcade
6 Field Trip
7 Gypsy World
8 Highest Score
9 Cardassian Imps
#10 Space Camp
#11 Day of Honor: Honor Bound
#12 Trapped in Time

Star Trek: Voyager
STARFLEET ACADEMY

#1 Lifeline
#2 The Chance Factor
#3 Quarantine

Star Trek movie tie-ins

Star Trek Generations
Star Trek First Contact
Star Trek Insurrection

Available from MINSTREL Books

STAR TREK®
INSURRECTION™

A Young Adult novelization
by John Vornholt
Based on the story by
Rick Berman
& Michael Piller
Screenplay by
Michael Piller

A MINSTREL® BOOK

Published by POCKET BOOKS
New York   London   Toronto   Sydney   Tokyo   Singapore

This book is a work of fiction. Names, characters, places and incidents are products of the author's imagination or are used fictitiously. Any resemblance to actual events or locales or persons, living or dead, is entirely coincidental.

A MINSTREL PAPERBACK *Original*

A Minstrel Book published by
POCKET BOOKS, a division of Simon & Schuster Inc.
1230 Avenue of the Americas, New York, NY 10020

STAR TREK is a Registered Trademark of Paramount Pictures.

A VIACOM COMPANY

This book is published by Pocket Books, a division of Simon & Schuster Inc., under exclusive license from Paramount Pictures.

ISBN: 0-671-02107-9

First Minstrel Books printing December 1998

10 9 8 7 6 5 4 3 2 1

A MINSTREL BOOK and colophon are registered trademarks of Simon & Schuster Inc.

Printed in the U.S.A.

For Neil the Rocker

CHAPTER 1

Artim loved to play hide-and-seek with his play-mates in the rows of freshly cut hay. The haystacks formed walls and mazes that stretched across the farmland all the way to the village and the open-air marketplace.

The piles of grain were supposed to protect the newly planted vegetables from the wind and birds. To the children, they became a magical land of forts, palaces, and caves, all waiting to be explored.

Artim was twelve years old, and the patterns on his skin were still emerging, growing darker. The Ba'ku community numbered only six hundred people, and everyone did his share of the work. Still, they understood that life was long, and there was much time to be grown-up. So they let the children play.

His friends ran past him, laughing, and Artim buried his head back under the hay. It smelled musty and ripe, and the prickly scent nearly made him sneeze. He wished his father, Sojef, and the other adults didn't have to work so hard. Everyone should be playing on a beautiful day like this.

Artim stuck his head out of the hay and looked around. On a far hillside, their milk animals grazed peacefully, getting fat. Soon it would be summer, and he and the other boys would herd them to the high plateaus. They would get skinny again on that trip, but they would grow their winter coats faster in the mountains.

Nestled against a rock wall in a large clearing was their village. The banners and pennants of the marketplace glittered like confetti against the rolling foothills and the sparkling sky.

Artim saw Anij, walking across the field, heading for the market. A spokesperson for the village, she looked strong and beautiful, as usual, and he wanted to follow her and see what she was doing. She smiled and greeted people as she walked. Everyone liked Anij—

Phsss . . .

Artim whirled in the direction of the strange sound, but he didn't see the shadow. Lately the boy had seen strange things from the corner of his eye, things like ghosts—or visions. But they didn't seem evil, just someone watching.

"There he is!" cried one of Artim's playmates, pointing at the boy in the haystack.

2

He laughed and scrambled from his hiding place, the noise forgotten. With his playmates in giddy pursuit, Artim scampered up a trail into the rocky foothills.

Panting and laughing, the boy ran along the twisted path; he jumped over the ruts and streams. Artim could hear his friends gaining on him, calling his name.

He ran toward the lake, thinking he could hide by the dam. Just as he spied the shimmering water through the trees, a bolt of lightning crackled across the sky.

A huge explosion rocked the peaceful countryside, and dirt and debris rained down upon Artim and his friends from the rocks above. *What is happening?* Some of the children on the path began to cry, and all of them scrambled for cover.

Artim was brave, because he was worried about his village. They didn't have any enemies, and no material that would explode like that. He jumped to his feet and began to run—even faster—back to his home.

What Artim *didn't* see was a strange man in a bulky suit, who charged down from the foothills, running stiffly. He was also headed for the village. Artim didn't see the armed men in pursuit either, but he knew when they fired their weapons at the fleeing figure.

The ground beneath him shook again, and the force propelled Artim onto his back and covered him with grimy dirt. When he sat up, the air was as hot as Anij's oven, and his skin felt all prickly.

Another bright plasma explosion ripped up the countryside, closer to the village. Panic set in, and people rushed in all directions. Artim could hear their screams. Despite the danger, he had to reach his father and the others!

Artim put his head down and dashed through the smoke and dust, racing toward his village.

"Hold your fire!" shouted Gallatin, the ranking Son'a officer on the observation team. Like all Son'a, a hood covered the back of his head.

Curtis, an experienced Starfleet lieutenant, looked back at him. Gallatin's skin was stretched so tightly that it looked as if his whole face would snap. Anger only made him more stressed, but he had good reason to be angry at the moment.

They both turned to look out the observation window of the duck blind, a hidden post situated in the rock wall behind the village. It was cloaked, and so were the field researchers—for the moment. Everything had been going so smoothly, until the android had gone berserk.

Of course, thought the lieutenant, *we were warned about this region of space.*

Gallatin scowled at her. "Try to get through to him!"

"Yes, sir," answered Curtis, plying her comm panel. "Base to Commander Data."

The android's halting, strangled voice answered, "Rerouting . . . microhydraulic . . . power distribution . . . regulating . . . thermal . . . overload."

Through the specially treated observation window she had seen him clearly, running awkwardly in the bulky isolation suit toward the village, past a young native boy. Curtis knew the boy would not know the android was beside him, thanks to the special suit Data wore which made him, and all the observers, invisible to the natives. Data was closer now to the duck blind, and Curtis could see that the android looked disoriented.

"Data," she ordered sternly, "Report to base immediately." *Come on, Data,* she thought. *Don't reveal yourself to them!*

His only response was more mumbling. "Transferring . . . positronic . . . matrix functions . . . engaging . . . secondary protocols."

The android started jerking on his helmet, as if he were smothering inside it.

"He's trying to remove the headpiece!" shouted one of the Son'a officers.

Oh, no! Curtis knew this would render the android visible to even the natives.

Gallatin growled, "All field units, intercept the android!"

Through the calibrated screen, Curtis could see the other officers in cloaked suits converging on Data. With any luck, if they got to him before he removed his helmet, they could drag him off without the villagers being any the wiser.

Although a dozen of them jumped on Data, they went flying off just as quickly. With his superhuman strength, he tossed the officers off his back as if they were rag dolls.

We're in trouble now, decided Curtis.

* * *

Artim finally found his father, Sojef, who was trying to guard his stall in the marketplace. Just as the boy reached Sojef, something big splashed into the little pond near him. Artim could see the ripples and splashing, as some invisible creature struggled out of the water.

"Father!" he shouted. "What's going on?"

Sojef just shrugged at the boy and held him tightly. He motioned to the other villagers. "Get inside . . . find shelter!"

Something moved beside Artim—something in the corner of his eye. *Just like before* . . . He turned to see a head suddenly materialize in midair.

"Aaagh!" screamed the boy as he jumped back.

His father grabbed Artim and held him away from the eerie golden head. Suddenly another invisible creature attacked the head—Artim could see red sparks flying between them. The head-creature then seemed to rip something from the other creature and he, too, became visible.

The man flew through the air and smashed to the ground. He blinked on and off, finally staying visible—an alien in a bulky suit.

That was when the floating head turned to look at Artim. There was strangeness but also kindness in those pale eyes. Before Artim could see more, Sojef pulled him away.

"Secondary protocols . . . active," said the stranger. He craned his neck, and Artim could see a burn wound on his neck. It wasn't bleeding, just burned.

6

More ripping sounded as the head tore off the rest of his suit. With every piece of clothing he shed, more of the alien became visible, until he stood before them in a black and purple uniform.

The gold stranger grabbed a weapon from the man on the ground. The Ba'ku ran shrieking for cover, but Artim couldn't move. He watched in awe as the stranger turned and aimed his weapon at the rock wall behind the village.

He shot a burst of fire, and something in the rock exploded with a red flash. *It wasn't the rock,* thought Artim. *Rock doesn't burn like that.* His father grabbed him and tried to pull him away from the madman.

"No, wait!" shouted Artim, struggling. "Look!"

They both watched as the rock face shimmered like something electronic—then it disappeared, revealing a very large window. Behind the window were more aliens in uniforms and strange equipment. They scurried for cover, and Artim was reminded of the crawlers he found when he overturned a rock.

"What is it?" asked Sojef in amazement.

"Who are they?" demanded Anij, pushing her way through the crowd.

Artim didn't know the answers, but he was certain that the pale man with the yellow eyes knew. The man lowered his weapon, looking satisfied with his mysterious work.

CHAPTER 2

The *Enterprise*-E, a Sovereign-class starship, orbited a planet of great seas and lush landmasses. The ship's oval saucer section gave the ship a more forward thrust than its predecessors. The *Enterprise* seemed poised for action, like a silver raptor coiled to leap.

In his quarters, Captain Jean-Luc Picard struggled with the collar of his jacket. *Blasted thing is supposed to fasten on a dress uniform.* His fingers fumbled with the four shiny pips, making sure they were all clasped properly.

Finally Dr. Beverly Crusher reached over to help him. "Allow me, Captain," she said with a smile.

"Thank you," answered Picard with relief. He dropped his hands to his sides and let someone with nimble fingers take over.

Counselor Deanna Troi hovered at the captain's elbow, waving a padd crammed with information. "We're running late, so let's keep at it. The population of Evora is three hundred million."

"Say the greeting again," said Picard, thinking they would be the first words from his mouth when he met the planet's delegates.

Troi nodded, taking her task seriously. With her charming accent, she intoned, "Yew-cheen chef-faw. Emphasis on the 'cheen' and the 'faw.'"

Before he could practice it, Beverly yanked tightly on his collar, nearly strangling him. "You either need a new uniform or a new neck."

Picard peered briefly into the mirror. Certainly there was some wrinkled skin around his neck. But he was still slim and fit—not bad for a man his age with an artificial heart.

"Yew-*cheen* chef-*faw*," he snapped. "My collar size is exactly the same as it was at the Academy."

Beverly smiled dryly. "Sure it is." Her strong fingers fastened his collar, brutally pinching his neck.

When the door chimed, Troi rushed to open it, letting in Will Riker, who was also dressed smartly in his best uniform.

The First Officer cringed as he reported, "Our guests have arrived . . . and are eating the floral arrangements on the banquet tables."

Crusher shrugged. "I guess they don't believe in cocktails before dinner."

Picard gripped the hem of his jacket and tugged it

into place. With a firm sense of duty and a pleasant smile, he marched out of his quarters, his officers hurrying to keep up with him.

"Are they vegetarians?" asked Troi with concern. She perused her padd. "That's not in the official report."

The captain said over his shoulder, "Better have the chef whip up a light balsamic vinaigrette . . . something that goes well with chrysanthemums. Yew-*cheen* chef-*faw*."

"Bridge to Captain Picard," came an insistent voice over his combadge.

The captain answered it. "Yes, Ensign Perim."

"Command wants to know our ETA at the Goren system."

"The Goren system?" asked Picard curiously. That had nothing to do with their current assignment.

Riker cleared his throat. "They need us to mediate some territorial dispute."

"We can't delay the archeological expedition to Hanoran Two," snapped Picard with frustration. "It would put us into the middle of monsoon season."

He skirted a pair of engineers who were working on a wall panel. There was hardly time to accomplish much-needed repairs, with Starfleet shunting them from one place to another.

Riker shrugged apologetically. "The Diplomatic Corps is busy with Dominion negotiations." They all knew the recent Dominion War had strained Starfleet's resources.

"So they need us to put out one more brushfire," muttered Picard. "Anyone remember when we used to be explorers?"

When no one cared to answer, Picard led them into the turbolift. "Yew-*cheen* chef-*faw*," he repeated to no one in particular.

Troi edged closer, still prepping the captain for the reception. "Remember, the Evora have a significantly less advanced technology than ours. They only achieved warp drive last year."

"A year?" asked Crusher. "And the Federation Council decided to make them a protectorate already?" Membership status in the Federation usually took much longer, with very strict application procedures.

Picard scowled. "In view of our losses to the Borg and the Dominion, the Council feels we need all the allies we can get these days."

The turbolift doors opened, and the captain faced a bustle of activity. Cheerful music spilled from the lounge, and Picard mustered a cheerful expression to go with it.

"You'll be expected to dance with Regent Cuzar," Troi reminded him.

"Can she mambo?" asked Beverly.

"Very funny," whispered the captain.

Wistfully, Crusher added, "Your captain used to cut quite a rug—"

Picard hurried away from the discussion of his youthful escapades. In the corridor, several officers in dress uniforms moved to make room for him and his staff.

"Captain on deck!" announced one young ensign.

Picard kept smiling and moving through the large crowd. His combadge sounded again, and Geordi La Forge's voice cut through the chatter. "La Forge to Picard. Captain, I need to talk to you before you go into the reception."

Before the captain could respond, he ran into Worf among the officers. "Captain—" began the Klingon.

"Worf, what are you doing here?" asked Picard with surprise.

"I was in the Manzar colony, installing a new defense perimeter, when I heard the *Enterprise* was in this sector."

The captain was distracted by Riker trying to explain to La Forge why this wasn't a good time to talk. "Have him come to the reception," Picard instructed his first officer, not breaking stride. "We'll talk here."

Riker nodded, and the captain turned back to his old comrade, Worf. "Stop by my quarters later. I have a few ideas about Manzar security."

They entered the banquet room, with Picard feeling as if he were being pulled in ten different directions. He heard Riker still talking urgently to La Forge, but then he was engulfed in the crowd and the music.

As a string quartet played a lively waltz, the sea of officers and dignitaries parted before the captain. Troi steered him efficiently toward Regent Cuzar and her delegation of eight extremely short aliens. Picard bowed his head toward her in an attempt to make himself shorter.

"Yew-*cheen* chef-*faw,* Regent Cuzar," he said impeccably. "Welcome aboard the *Enterprise.*"

The Evoran dignitary smiled with delight. "Captain Picard, may I welcome you in the time-honored tradition of my people."

She motioned, and an aide stepped forward with an exquisite but bulky headpiece. Picard feared the worst—that he would have to wear it—and his fears were confirmed. Regent Cuzar held the headpiece toward him, and he bent down even lower to allow her to place it on his head.

"We are so honored to be accepted within the great Federation family."

Picard straightened and nodded bravely, trying not to imagine how silly he looked in the ceremonial crown.

The regent allowed him to escape. "Please, I know you have other guests to greet."

"We have a dance later, I believe?" added the captain.

"I look forward to it." The regent walked away, surrounded by her ministers.

Picard turned to Troi. "Counselor?" He indicated the headpiece. *What am I supposed to do with this?* he wondered. *How long do I leave it on?*

"Nice beadwork" was her only comment.

Before Troi could advise him of the protocol for

this prickly situation, they were interrupted by Geordi La Forge. The Chief Engineer pushed his padd into Picard's hands. "Excuse me, sir. This message came in from Admiral Dougherty. He's aboard a Son'a ship in Sector Four-four-one. He's requesting Data's schematics."

"Is something wrong?" asked Troi, overhearing them.

"The message doesn't say," answered Geordi.

Picard frowned with concern and kept his voice low. "Data should have been back by now. They were only scheduled to observe the Ba'ku village for a week."

He turned to Geordi. "Set up a secured comm link to the admiral in the anteroom."

"Yes, sir."

Geordi moved away, and Picard was about to follow him when a Bolian science officer grabbed him by the arm. "Captain, Hars Adislo. We met at the Nel Bato Conference last year. Did you ever have a chance to read my paper on thermionic transconductance?"

The captain smiled painfully, not remembering a thing about the Bolian or his paper. He was relieved a few moments later when La Forge notified him that the comm link was active.

"Excuse me," said Picard, rushing away and removing his headpiece.

The captain entered a small anteroom off the banquet hall and looked at a viewscreen. The face of

Admiral Matthew Dougherty glowered at him. Behind the admiral were the unfamiliar sights and crew of a Son'a ship.

"Data is not acknowledging any Starfleet protocols," complained Dougherty. "Not responding to any of our hails."

"You have no idea what precipitated his behavior?" asked Picard.

The admiral shook his head. "And now he and the Ba'ku are holding our people hostage down there."

"The *Enterprise* can be at your position in two days," promised Picard.

"That's probably not a good idea," grumbled Dougherty. "Your ship hasn't been fitted for this region of space; there are environmental concerns."

"What kind of concerns?"

"We haven't fully identified the anomalies yet," explained the admiral. "They're calling this whole area 'the Briar Patch.' It took us a day to reach a location where we could get a signal out to you. Just get me Data's schematics. I'll keep you informed."

Picard nodded, worried about his unique comrade.

"Dougherty out."

The screen switched back to the Federation seal, and Picard turned to La Forge. "Send him the schematics."

"Yes, sir," answered Geordi with a sigh.

"Ensign!" called Picard to the young officer guarding the door.

He popped inside the door. "Sir?"

"Report to the galley, and tell the chef to skip the fish course."

The ensign looked puzzled for a moment, but an order was an order.

As he hurried off, Picard turned to Geordi. "I want our guests to depart as quickly as etiquette allows. I'll ask Worf to delay his return to DS9, so he can join us. We're going to stop by Sector Four-four-one on our way to the Goren system."

La Forge gave him a curious smile. "They are in *opposite* directions, sir."

"Are they?" asked Picard innocently.

With a grin, Geordi headed out of the anteroom, leaving the captain to gather his thoughts. There had been enough diplomacy and cleaning up of messes— and far too much war. Captain Picard was ready for adventure of another sort—almost any other sort.

He couldn't think of any job more urgent than protecting Data. Nobody understood the android like his own crew.

With a scowl, Picard put the ornate headpiece back on his head, mustered a smile, and strode into the banquet hall.

The Son'a spaceship cruised through ghostly tendrils of glowing plasma and dust. They resembled the stingers of a giant jellyfish, trying to ensnare the graceful craft. In the distance, a ringed panet was visible through the wispy clouds. It looked trapped by the forces of the universe.

Inside the ship on an observation deck was a beautiful salon. It was called the Body Enhancement Facility, and Son'a men and women lay on the massage tables, with Tarlac and Elloran attendants working on them.

Admiral Dougherty paced uncomfortably. As many times as he saw it, the skin-pulling and dialysis machines of the Son'a rejuvenation process made him squirm. As their skin stretched and was smoothed with fluids, laser surgery, and makeup, his own skin crawled. But it wasn't his place as a Starfleet officer to criticize alien behavior. After all, it wasn't as if humans were immune to such vanity.

The admiral had to admit that the extravagant costumes of the Son'a, with all the different fabrics, feathers, and jewels, were wonderful. The Son'a took a pride in their appearance that he found refreshing. So what if they tried to prolong their youthful looks? They might as well make use of the technology.

Even as he told himself this, he looked away. The skin-stretching process still unsettled him.

"Admiral Dougherty," said a voice with a sneer in it.

"Yes." He turned to look at Ru'afo, the ahdar, or commander, of the Son'a forces. The two most beautiful attendants worked on Ru'afo, which showed his importance as much as anything. They gently massaged creams and oils into his plumped and soothed skin.

"I never should have let you talk me into the duck blind in the first place," complained the Son'a commander.

The admiral stiffened in his crisp uniform, trying to maintain some dignity in this place. *Alien alliances are always tough,* he told himself. *Best to hold my tongue.*

"Your Federation procedures have made this mission ten times as difficult as it needed to be," said Ru'afo.

Dougherty stuck his chin out. "Our procedures were in place to protect the planet's population from unnecessary risk."

"Six hundred people!" scoffed the Son'a. "Do you want to avoid unnecessary risks? Next time, leave your android home."

A voice echoed over a nearby comm panel: *"Bridge to Ahdar Ru'afo. We're approaching the planet."*

The Son'a commander motioned to his attendants to hurry; then he pressed his comm link and said, "Take us into a high orbit."

"Yes, sir."

Ru'afo rose from his chair and motioned to Dougherty. "Lie down, Admiral. The girls will take twenty years off your face."

"Another time," muttered the admiral, trying not to show his distaste.

"Your self-restraint puzzles me, Admiral," said

Ru'afo, admiring his own face in the mirror. "You continue to deny yourself every benefit this mission has to offer."

Dougherty shrugged. "I prefer to wait until we can share the benefits with all the people of the Federation."

Suddenly the ship was rocked by a blast that staggered the admiral and the Son'a. As everyone talked at once, Ru'afo scowled and stalked out of the salon. Dougherty hurried to keep up.

A few moments later, they emerged on the bridge of the Son'a ship. Purple alert lights were flashing, and frantic beeps sounded in the air. Two Son'a officers remained calm at their stations, their faces masks of stretched skin. Tarlac and Elloran officers manned the rest of the stations.

"Report," demanded Ru'afo.

"Phaser blast. Unknown origin," replied the Son'a on the helm.

"Raise shields," ordered Ru'afo as another blast shook the starship. "Take us out of orbit."

Before that command could be carried out, a Tarlac officer shouted, "Photon torpedoes. Brace for impact!"

A swift succession of jolts knocked Dougherty off his feet, and smoke began to pour from an auxiliary instrument panel. *If we don't do something to stop this attack, we're in serious trouble!* But he was a guest on this ship, so he could only stand aside while Ru'afo ordered his crew to prepare for the attack.

A flat computer voice reported, "Warning. Outer hull damage, deck three."

"Visual contact!" said the Elloran on ops.

All their attention was riveted on the viewscreen. They saw a small but powerful warship emerge from gas clouds looking like a shark rising from the depths. *It's a Federation scout ship,* thought Dougherty with alarm.

"That's *our* ship!" he gasped.

The sleek vessel unleashed one final burst of fire as it sped past the floundering Son'a ship. In the forward cockpit, Dougherty could almost see him—*It's that crazed android!*

CHAPTER
3

The *Enterprise* sped through the starscape, little more than a blur at warp speed.

The delegates having departed and the ship now under way, Picard relished a few minutes alone in his quarters, where he coud grab a cup of tea and a bite to eat. He would still be working, as he had a lot to read in order to get up to speed on the Ba'ku projcct and the area of space known as "the Briar Patch."

It helped to have the soothing strains of Beethoven's Sonata *Pathetique,* First Movement, playing in the background. The captain rose from his chair and loosened the collar of his dress uniform. Then he strode to the food replicator.

"Tea. Earl Grey. Hot." The tea materialized on the

tray, and Picard picked it up and gingerly took a sip. *Ah . . .* He felt civilized again, capable of absorbing a paddful of information.

Needing more room, Picard crossed to his dining table and sat down. The table was covered with more padds, charts and graphs, and a set of transparent maps. He also had to confront his half-eaten salad and a stale roll.

Have to eat while I have the chance, decided Picard. He thought about the irony of attending a banquet and getting nothing to eat. If he worked fast, he could eat, drink, and read at the same time.

The captain speared a forkful of salad with one hand and balanced his teacup with the other. Between these maneuvers, Picard nudged his padd around the table, trying to find a spot to prop it up.

The report mentioned so many bizarre features about the Briar Patch that he soon realized he would need his charts. Trying to juggle everything, Picard reached across the table and grabbed a chart. Pulling it back, he accidentally caught it on his salad plate and dumped the salad into his lap.

Picard scowled at the Gorgonzola dressing congealing on his jacket. Of course, at that moment a chime sounded at his door.

"Who is it?" he muttered.

An amplified voice answered, "Commander Riker."

The captain looked at himself and shrugged. His

first officer had seen him in worse condition than this. "Come! Computer, end music."

The door opened as the music stopped, and Will Riker strode in, another padd in his hand. He glanced at Picard's stained jacket.

"I'm a casualty of a working lunch," explained the captain. He took off his jacket and grabbed his regular cranberry tunic.

"I've been going over the few star charts we have of the Briar Patch," said Picard, pushing the page under Riker's nose. "It's full of supernova remnants, false vacuum fluctuations—"

"And Gorgonzola cheese," remarked Riker, flicking a whitish chunk off the chart.

"We won't be able to go any faster than one-third impulse in that muck," grumbled the captain. "Now I see why communications are so bad."

Riker handed him his padd. "Nothing dangerous turned up in the astrometric survey."

As the captain studied the readouts, he scratched his chin, puzzled. "So where are the 'environmental concerns' the admiral was talking about?"

The first officer shrugged. "The only unusual readings were low levels of metaphasic radiation from interstellar dust across the region."

Worf's deep voice sounded over the comm panel. *"Bridge to Captain Picard. We are approaching Sector Four-four-one."*

"Slow to impulse," ordered Picard. "We're on our way."

When they emerged on the bridge a few moments later, the viewscreen commanded their attention. The shifting clouds and strands of the Briar Patch were like an immense, messy web. They could only plow through it, dodging the most deadly parts.

He strode around the circular bridge, satisfied with the crew on duty. Kell Perim, a female Trill, was at the conn. Deanna Troi sat in the command chair, Worf was at tactical, and Geordi La Forge was at ops.

"We're about to lose communications with Starfleet, Captain," warned La Forge.

Picard glanced at Deanna. "Do you have everything you need from Command?"

"We've downloaded all the files on the duck-blind mission, as well as intelligence reports on the Son'a."

"You have two days to become experts," said the captain, his gaze taking in everyone on the bridge. "Mr. Worf, your job—and mine—will be to find a plan to safely capture Data."

The Klingon held up a tricorder. "I've already asked Commander La Forge to modify a tricorder with one of Data's actuation servos. Its operational range is only seven meters, but it should shut him down."

Picard nodded, pleased with the Klingon's initiative. "It's good to have you back, Worf. Conn, slow to one-third. Take us in."

Slowing down to a cautious crawl, the *Enterprise* entered the ghostly tendrils of the Briar Patch.

* * *

The *Enterprise*-E had a vast library made up of computer texts, charts and graphs, and regular books. Every shred of information known to the Federation was in here somewhere, on a shelf or an isolinear chip.

Deanna Troi liked to explore the library, delving into psychology cases, field reports, and whatever caught her attention. But today was no time for leisurely surfing. As the captain had told them, they had to be experts on the Son'a and Ba'ku in a matter of hours.

So Deanna Troi and Will Riker sat side by side at matching computer terminals, reading the data they had received from Starfleet. There were a few people at other stations, plus a stern-faced librarian who ran a tight command.

After reading pages of reports and memos, she summed it up for Riker. "The Son'a discovered an M-class planet with humanoid life—the Ba'ku—six months ago. Turned out it's in Federation space, so they came to us to get approval for a sociological study. The Federation Council suggested it be a joint mission."

"Why was Data assigned?" asked Will.

"Environmental concerns again," she answered, reading right from the report. "An android could be safely exposed to the elements during the installation of a duck blind."

"Sssshhh!" hissed a voice, and Deanna turned to see the librarian glaring at them.

Troi went back to her reading, but she felt nervous, as if she were missing something. She took a page of paper from a small notepad, tore off a corner, and wadded it up to make a paper ball.

Riker studied his screen, then whispered, "I don't see anything to suggest the Son'a have any interest in sociology."

"What are they interested in?" asked Deanna.

"Wine, women, and song."

She smiled slyly. "You should feel right at home with them."

When Riker ignored her, she threw her ball of paper and hit him on the head. When he stared at her, she looked innocently at her screen.

Will began to roll a little paper ball himself. "They're nomadic—collectors of precious metals and jewels."

"Hmm, I should feel right at home with them, too," joked Troi.

"You're in luck," said Riker. "They use alien women as indentured servants. A half century ago, they conquered two primitive races, the Tarlac and the Ellora. They integrated them into their culture as a labor class."

He lifted his right hand and was about to throw his paper ball back at her when the librarian walked by. She gazed at them suspiciously, as if knowing they were troublemakers.

Riker turned sheepishly back to his computer screen. "Look at this."

Troi rose from her chair and peered over Riker's broad shoulder. He pointed out a few items. "The Son'a are known to have produced mass quantities of the narcotic ketracel-white. Their ships are rumored to be equipped with isolytic subspace weapons outlawed by the Second Khitomer Accord."

"Why would we be involved with these people?" asked Deanna.

"Good question."

They exchanged a brief glance that had nothing to do with the Son'a, but more to do with being so close to each other. As Will returned to the computer screen, Deanna reached over to tuck an errant lock of dark hair under his collar. She paused for a moment, twisting the hair into a curl.

"You haven't done that in a long time," said Riker.

"What?" She feigned ignorance, but she knew what he was talking about. She really had no idea what had come over her in the last few minutes—except that she had never stopped caring for her old flame Will.

"What you're doing to my neck," he said with amusement.

"Was I doing something to your neck?" Deanna smiled innocently and pulled her hand away.

With a frown, Riker stopped the scrolling information on the screen and leaned forward to read it. "It says here that some form of genetic anomaly has prevented the Son'a from procreating."

"No children?" asked Troi with interest.

"If that's true, they're a dying race." Riker jerked

suddenly as a tiny paper ball hit him in the neck. "Hey!"

Deanna turned around and saw an ensign sitting at a nearby computer station. He seemed to be suppressing a laugh as he stared intently at his screen. She also saw the librarian glaring at her and Will.

"He started it," she said, pointing at the First Officer.

"I didn't do anything, I swear it," protested Will.

She grabbed his hand and pulled him toward the door, suppressing a giddy laugh. *This is almost like being a kid again.*

Captain Picard paced the bridge of the *Enterprise* as the graceful ship moved carefully through the Briar Patch. He glanced at the tactical station, where Lieutenant Nara was ten minutes into double-shift, because his relief hadn't shown up.

Picard sat in the command chair and tapped the comm panel on the arm. "Bridge to Commander Worf."

When there wasn't an immediate answer, he repeated, more loudly, "Worf?"

"Captain . . ." came a drowsy voice.

"I don't know how they do it on Deep Space Nine, but on the *Enterprise,* we still report for duty on time."

"Yes, sir. I . . . I must have slept through my alarm. I'm on my way."

"We'll skip the court-martial this time," said Picard with sympathy.

He cocked his head and listened to the sound of his ship. Something was wrong, minutely wrong, but wrong nevertheless. He stood and walked over to La Forge on ops and Perim at the conn.

"When was the last time we aligned our torque sensors?" he asked.

"Two months ago, sir," answered Ensign Perim.

"They don't sound right," declared the captain.

La Forge and Perim glanced at each other and set to work on their consoles. Picard knew he could easily be wrong, but he didn't think he was.

Geordi nodded, clearly impressed. "The torque sensors *are* out of alignment . . . by twelve microns. You could hear that?"

The captain smiled wistfully. "When I was an ensign, I could detect a *three*-micron misalignment."

"Excuse me, sir," said Nara at tactical. "The Son'a ship with Admiral Dougherty aboard has entered tracking range."

"Try to hail them," ordered Picard.

Worf stomped onto the bridge, looking embarrassed, uncombed, and unkempt. He moved quietly toward the tactical station.

Nara reported, "Admiral Dougherty responding."

Worf took the young officer's place, and Picard shot him a look. "Straighten your baldric, Commander. On screen."

With a tug of his sash, the Klingon put the images of Admiral Dougherty and a resplendent Son'a on the viewscreen. From his reading, Picard assumed that the Son'a was the ahdar, Ru'afo. *His quarters are opulently decorated for a spaceship,* thought Picard.

The admiral scowled. "Captain, I wasn't expecting you."

"This was too important for the *Enterprise* to be on the sidelines, Admiral."

Dougherty shook his head gravely. "I wish I had better news. Commander Data attacked us in the mission scout ship yesterday. Ru'afo and I have decided to send in an assault team."

"Sir," said the captain with concern, "Commander Worf and I have been working on several tactical plans to safely—"

"Your android has turned dangerously violent, Captain," the Son'a snapped at him. "Considerable damage was done to my ship. He must be destroyed."

The admiral gave a heavy sigh. "I know what Data means to Starfleet, Jean-Luc, but our crew is at the mercy of those people on the planet."

"If our first attempt to capture Data fails, I will terminate him," promised Picard. "I should be the one to do it. I'm his captain . . . and his friend."

Dougherty paused to consider the offer, but Ru'afo scoffed at Picard. "It isn't safe for you to remain in this area."

"He's right," admitted the admiral. "Our shields

30

have been upgraded to protect against the environmental anomalies."

"We haven't noticed any ill effects," replied the captain.

Dougherty frowned in thought, weighing Picard's request. "All right, you have twelve hours. Then I want you out of the Briar Patch. In the meantime, we'll be heading out to the perimeter to call for Son'a reinforcements, in case you fail."

"Understood," answered Picard, his jaw set with determination. *Twelve hours to save Data. Is it enough?*

"Good luck." The admiral didn't sound as if he believed in luck. "Dougherty out."

CHAPTER
4

A Starfleet shuttlecraft cruised cautiously through the eerie gas clouds of the Briar Patch. When they finally emerged into normal space, Picard breathed a sigh of relief and relaxed at the controls. He could see their destination—a large ringed planet glowing in the distance.

"Sensors are not picking up any ships coming from the surface," reported Worf, the only other person in the shuttlecraft.

"Transmit a wide variety co-variant signal. That will get his attention."

Worf obeyed, then said, "He might be using the planet's rings to mask his approach."

"The metaphasic radiation in those rings is in extreme flux. Steer clear of them, Mr. Worf." The captain peered out the cockpit window. "Come out, come out, wherever you are."

"Sir?" asked Worf.

"Oh, it's just something my mother used to—" Without warning they were slammed by a phaser blast.

"Hold on!" Picard grabbed the controls and sent the shuttlecraft into a sharp climb. "Open hailing frequencies."

After Worf had done so, the captain pleaded, "Data, this is Captain Picard. Please acknowledge."

They were rocked by another phaser blast. Picard took desperate evasive maneuvers, but phasers slammed their ship at every turn. His actions and decisions were always slower than the android's.

"Sir," said Worf, "if we fire a tachyon burst, it may force him to reset his shield harmonics. When he does, we could beam him out."

"Make it so," ordered Picard.

When the scout ship swooped back into range, Worf pushed his controls. The Klingon smiled with satisfaction as the tachyon beam connected with the larger ship.

"Beam him out," ordered Picard.

The Klingon shook his head as he worked his console. "He's activated a transport inhibitor." They couldn't beam the android out.

"Prepare to enter the atmosphere. We'll use the ionospheric boundary to lose him!" The captain worked hard to stabilize the ship, but another phaser blast sent them reeling toward the planet.

Through the window, the captain could see the scout ship zoom past them, trying to cut them off. "He can fly a ship, so his brain is obviously functioning. Threats don't work . . ." He trailed off as he thought about the android he'd worked with for so long. "I wonder how well he responds to music. Mr. Worf, do you know Gilbert and Sullivan?"

"I'm sorry, sir, but I haven't had time to meet all of the new crew members—"

"No, Mr. Worf. The nineteenth-century composers, Gilbert and Sullivan. Mr. Data was rehearsing a part in their operetta *H.M.S. Pinafore . . .*"

As Worf looked on with puzzlement, Captain Picard bellowed a verse:

"His nose should pant, and his lip should curl. His cheeks should flame and his brow should furl—"

Data's voice immediately chirped in over the comm. *"His bosom should heave, and his heart should glow. And his fist should be ready for a knock-down blow!"*

Picard signaled Worf, who joined in as the three of them sang it again. When they finally rested after the last bellicose note, Picard and Worf both gazed at their instruments.

"He's stopped firing," said the captain with relief.

But the android hadn't stopped singing as he finished the number by himself.

"Prepare the docking clamps," whispered Picard.

Worf obeyed, and Picard piloted them close enough to the scout ship to latch on with docking clamps. At once the singing stopped and the scout ship acted like a harpooned whale, rocking back and forth to shake off the smaller ship.

As Picard and Worf were bounced around the cockpit, Worf shouted, "Sir, inertial coupling is exceeding tolerance! If we don't release him, he may destroy both vessels."

"I'm not letting go of him," vowed Picard.

Lashed together, the two ships spiraled to the planet surface. "Warning," said the computer, "impact with surface in twenty seconds."

"Reroute emergency power to inertial dampers," ordered Picard.

Worf tried, but he couldn't. "The damping sequencer was damaged by phaser fire."

"Transferring controls to manual!" said Picard, working feverishly.

"Warning: impact with surface in ten seconds," announced the computer.

The captain plied his controls, trying to ignore the ground looming ever closer.

"Damping field established!" barked Worf.

Picard applied maximum power as the small shuttle gained control of the descent. Both ships swept into a trajectory parallel with the ground and then finally headed back up into space.

A few seconds later Worf popped the hatch leading

from the shuttle to the scout ship. He found Data sitting in the pilot's chair, a confused look on his face.

Without warning, Data lunged toward the Klingon, who jumped back and pushed a button on his modified tricorder. The android froze in midair, and he dropped to the deck only a few inches away from Worf.

"Captain," said the Klingon with relief, "Commander Data is in custody."

After the *Enterprise* arrived in orbit, Captain Picard, Dr. Crusher, and Counselor Troi beamed down to the planet. They brought a work crew with them to disassemble the duck blind.

The captain was ready for anything, so he drew his phaser as he walked toward the village. But it was the strangest "hostage" situation he ever saw.

The Ba'ku, who appeared to be a simple people, sat at wooden tables with the Starfleet personnel they were supposedly holding hostage. They were all eating a sumptuous meal and talking cheerfully. At separate tables sat the Son'a crew; even they seemed to be having a good time. It was like a picnic.

Laughter startled Picard, and he turned to see several children playing a juggling game with colorful objects. The dexterity and hand-eye coordination required for this game was amazing, far beyond what human children could do.

When the hostages saw the captain and his team, they stopped speaking and seemed almost disappointed to see them. The conversation died down, and a Son'a officer and a Starfleet lieutenant rose to greet them.

"Captain, Subahdar Gallatin, Son'a Command," said the man with the stretched, artificial-looking skin.

"Lieutenant Curtis, attaché to Admiral Dougherty," replied the female officer.

"Are you all right?" Picard asked the lieutenant.

"We've been treated extremely well by these people," answered Curtis.

The children went back to their game, and Deanna Troi watched them closely. "They have an incredible clarity of perception, Captain. I've never encountered a species with such mental discipline."

Several of the Ba'ku were now headed their way. In the lead was an attractive woman, followed by two males in simple clothing. One of the children stopped to gaze at the man in the lead, and Picard guessed they were father and son.

"My name is Sojef, Captain," said the Ba'ku man.

"Jean-Luc Picard. My officers, Dr. Crusher and Counselor Troi." They nodded politely but warily to the Ba'ku.

"Would you like something to eat?" asked Sojef.

"No, we're here to . . . rescue them," admitted Picard.

"As you wish," said Sojef with disappointment. "But I would ask you to disarm yourselves. This village is a sanctuary of life."

With a glance at the peaceful scene, Picard holstered his phaser. He turned to Crusher and Troi and said, "Prepare to transport the hostages to the ship."

"They should be quarantined before joining the ship's population," said Crusher.

The captain nodded, and Crusher and Troi moved off to check the hostages. The work crew headed for the Starfleet duck blind, built into the rock wall. What had once been a marvel of engineering was now useless.

Seeing the reluctance on the hostages' faces, Picard felt guilty. "We were under the impression they were being held against their will."

The woman looked shocked. "It's not our custom to have guests here at all, let alone hold them against their will."

Picard gazed at the woman, sensing that she was passionate but also levelheaded. "What is your name?"

"Anij," she answered.

Sojef broke in, "The artificial life-form would not allow them to leave. He told us they were our enemies and more would follow."

"*Are* you our enemy?" asked Anij suspiciously.

Now it was Picard's turn to bristle. "My people have a strict policy of noninterference with other cultures. In fact, it's our Prime Directive."

"Your Prime Directive apparently doesn't include spying on other cultures," said Anij snidely.

The captain frowned. "If I were in your shoes, I'd feel the same way after what happened. And the artificial life-form is a member of our crew. Apparently, he became ill."

The second man spoke. "There did seem to be a phase variance in his positronic matrix that we were unable to repair."

Picard looked at the other man with surprise. Before he could say anything, Anij remarked, "I believe the captain finds it hard to believe that we'd have any skills repairing a positronic device."

Sojef smiled. "Our technological abilities aren't apparent because we've chosen not to employ them in our daily lives. We believe when you create a machine to do the work of a man, you take something away from the man."

"At one time, we explored the galaxy just as you do," added Anij.

"You have warp capability?" asked Picard.

"Capability, yes. But where can warp drive take us, except away from here?"

Picard looked around at the bucolic paradise. It was the kind of life to which everyone dreamed of escaping, at one time or another. As the Starfleet hostages reluctantly said good-bye to the Ba'ku, a humming-bird buzzed Picard's ear.

"I understand," said Picard with sympathy. "I apologize for our intrusion."

* * *

Back on the *Enterprise,* Picard hailed Admiral Dougherty on the Son'a ship. To the captain, it all seemed cut-and-dried. He told his superior, "Because they have warp capabilities, the consequences to their society are minimal."

"You've done a terrific job, Jean-Luc," said Dougherty. "Now pack your bags and get out of there. How's Data?"

"In stasis. La Forge is completing his diagnostic."

Dougherty nodded. "I'll need all your paperwork tomorrow. We're heading back your way. Set course to rendezvous with us, so you can transfer our crew and equipment on your way out."

"You're not finished here?" asked Picard with surprise.

"Just a few loose ends to tie up. Dougherty out."

The captain turned off the viewer and looked at his desk with its mess of padds, reports, and blinking screens. His eyes were pulled to his porthole, through which the peaceful, ringed planet shimmered warmly.

He didn't want to leave. Not only did he like it here, but he was also worried for the Ba'ku and their simple way of life. Even if the Federation's intentions were good, their blundering had endangered innocent people. The Ba'ku deserved to be left alone.

This is a special place, thought Picard. *How special maybe none of us realizes.*

CHAPTER
5

Unable to sit still, Captain Picard went down to engineering to see Geordi La Forge. The chief engineer showed him several small components which were burned beyond recognition.

"I took these out of Data's neural net," he explained. "They contain memory engrams."

"Do you know how they were damaged?"

"By a Son'a weapon," said Geordi with disapproval. "There's no doubt about it, sir—that's what made Data malfunction."

The captain looked doubtful. "The Son'a reports claim they didn't fire until *after* he malfunctioned."

"I don't believe it happened that way."

"Why would they fire at him without provocation?"

Geordi shrugged. "All I know is that he was functioning normally until he was shot, then his fail-safe system was activated."

"Fail-safe?" asked Picard.

"His ethical and moral subroutines took over all his basic functions."

"So you're saying he still knew the difference between right and wrong?"

Geordi nodded. "In a sense, that's *all* he knew. The system is designed to protect him against anyone who might try to take advantage of his memory loss."

"And yet he still attacked us," said Picard thoughtfully. "And told the Ba'ku we were a threat." *Why? Why would Data believe Starfleet is a threat to these people?*

Geordi rubbed his eyes as he studied his readouts. The captain noticed his discomfort and asked, "Implants bothering you?"

"It's nothing," insisted La Forge. "I'm just a little tired. Let's wake up our patient."

Geordi led the way to a door and punched a code into the security lock. The door slid back to reveal a small space in which Data was strapped to the bulkhead. Diagnostic devices monitored him, beeping and purring.

The android appeared to be asleep until La Forge touched a panel. Then he awoke, bright-eyed, and looked around.

"Captain, Geordi," said Data in greeting.

"You're aboard the *Enterprise,* Data," said Picard gently.

The android cocked his head focusing on an internal systems check. "I seem to be missing several memory engrams."

Geordi held them up for him to see. "Oh, there they are," said Data.

"What's the last thing you remember?" asked Picard.

Data sang, "His nose should pant and his lip should curl—"

"From the mission," added the captain.

"I was in an isolation unit, collecting physiometric data on Ba'ku children. My last memory is going into the hills, following a boy. After that, I possess no memory."

"We're going back," vowed Picard, "to find that boy."

While the adults talked, Artim sat on the ground, playing with his palm pet. It was a cute animal which one of the Starfleet people told him looked like a cross between a jellyfish and a caterpillar. Now the strangers from offland had come back and were talking to his father. He didn't know why they had come back, but he didn't trust them. Artim was only helping because his father had asked him to.

The boy kept looking at the stranger with the golden skin and yellow eyes—the artificial man.

Since he was the one who had gone crazy, Artim decided to watch him carefully.

Sojef put his hand on his son's shoulder. "Artim, do you remember where you were on the day of the lightning, when the artificial life-form appeared to us?"

The boy stood up and pointed. "In the hills, by the dam."

"Can you show us?" asked the captain, who looked stern but spoke gently.

Artim nodded and led the way into the foothills toward the lake. The strangers, his father, Anij, and other village leaders trailed behind him, and Captain Picard and Anij were the closest ones. He could hear their conversation.

"Haven't you disrupted our lives enough?" asked Anij.

"I understand how you feel," answered Picard with sympathy. "We just want to retrace Data's movements that day."

"Why?"

"I don't like to leave questions unanswered," replied Picard.

"Then you must spend your life answering questions." Holding her chin high, Anij strode away from the captain.

Artim saw the android, Data, looking at him. The boy grew afraid and wanted to run, but the strange life-form only stepped closer.

"There is no reason to fear me," Data said. "I am operating within normal parameters."

"What?"

"They fixed me."

Artim didn't care what they had done to him—he was still strange. His father put an arm around the boy and gave Data a look of warning. *Leave my boy alone* was the message.

The android turned with confusion to his captain. "The boy is afraid of me."

"It's nothing personal, Data. These people have rejected technology. And you—"

"I am the personification of everything they have rejected," said the android. "I do not believe I made a very good first impression."

Artim kept climbing into the rocky foothills, with the others following him. They came to a fast-moving brook, and he hopped across the damp stones. The captain also hopped across the stones, nearly slipping, but he looked like he was having fun.

The other adults stared at Picard as if he weren't acting his age. They walked across the brook on a narrow spit of sand, but Artim liked the way the captain did it.

The boy led them over a rise, and they came to a crystal blue lake, shimmering in a lush valley. An earthen dam kept the water from running into a large stream. Artim stared at the peaceful scene, trying to remember the day it had been chaotic.

The android lifted a boxlike instrument and trained it on the water. "Tricorder functions are limited due to heavy deposits of kelbonite in these hills."

"How about a passive radiation scan?" asked the captain.

Data adjusted his tricorder and frowned. "Curious. There appear to be strong neutrino emissions coming from the lake."

Artim and the others watched as Data strode to the edge of the lake. He continued to take tricorder readings, even as he began to wade into the water. The boy gasped when the strange being walked so far in that he disappeared *under* the water.

"Can he breathe underwater?" the boy asked the captain.

"Data doesn't breathe."

"Won't he rust?"

Picard smiled. "No."

The boy shook his head, marveling at the artificial man. He was beginning to see why the captain took such interest in Data—why he even treated him like a friend.

After a while, Data emerged from the lake, dripping and tracking mud and weeds. He read his tricorder as he walked toward them.

"Sir, I believe I know what is causing the neutrino emissions," he reported. "I can show you."

Picard nodded, and Data strode to the top of the earthen dam. He grabbed a heavy wheel that usually required two of the strongest people in the village to turn. The android twisted the wheel as if it were a toy, and the floodgates opened. Artim could hear the rushing water pouring out into the streambed.

"Are there any other machines like him in the offland?" Artim asked the captain.

Before he could reply, his father cut in, "The offland is no concern of yours, Artim."

The boy said nothing. He was willing to wait and watch the lake slowly drain. It wasn't long before he saw something strange in the shrinking lake—it shimmered with water flowing off, yet it was invisible! A bird landed at the top of the thing which wasn't there.

"A cloaked ship," said Captain Picard in surprise.

"It is clearly Federation in origin, Captain," added Data, striding toward them.

"They said they had just a few loose ends to tie up," muttered Picard angrily.

Anij rushed to grab a rowboat tied to a rickety wooden plank. Picard and Data followed her, and the three of them clambered into the boat.

"It might be wiser for you to stay on shore," Picard told Anij.

Her response was to grab an oar and push them away from the bank. Artim and his father watched as the three of them began to row toward the shimmering mirage in the lake.

Back on the *Enterprise,* Will Riker took a hail from Admiral Dougherty and Ru'afo, the Son'a commander. Being a Starfleet officer, he tried not to wince at the sight of the alien Ru'afo leaking green scum from the boils under his skin. Instead he looked at Admiral Dougherty. But that was painful, too, because the admiral was very angry.

"Why haven't you left orbit yet?" demanded Dougherty.

"Captain Picard is still on the surface, sir."

"Doing what?"

Riker answered, "He didn't want to leave until we could explain why Data malfunctioned. His future in Starfleet could depend on it."

The admiral scowled. "Remind the captain his twelve hours are up."

"Yes, sir," said Riker, snapping to attention.

"Dougherty out."

The viewscreen switched back to the Starfleet logo, and Riker scratched his chin. He couldn't help but feel there was something wrong with the Son'a and their constant facial manipulations. Either they were the most vain race in the quadrant, or the most unhealthy.

Either way, he didn't like their being in charge.

On the lake, Picard, Data, and Anij floated closer to the cloaked ship in their rowboat. Data worked his tricorder, and a hatch opened on the mysterious vessel. Picard drew his phaser, climbed onto the ship, and led the way through the open hatch.

A moment later they walked into a place that

shouldn't have existed, but did. It was the Ba'ku village.

Data studied his tricorder. "It is a holographic projection. Incomplete, I might add." The android pointed to a gap in the rock, where a patch of hologrid showed through.

The captain turned to Anij and said, "You're seeing a computer-driven image created by photons and forcefields."

"I know what a hologram is," answered the woman impatiently. "The question is, why would someone want to create one of our village?"

Picard turned grimly to Data. "If you were following the boy and discovered this ship—"

"It is conceivable I was shot to protect the secret of its existence."

The captain frowned. "Why create a duplicate village . . . except to deceive the Ba'ku."

"Deceive us?" asked Anij.

"To move you off this planet. You go to sleep one night in your village, and you wake up the next morning in this flying holodeck. A week or a month later, you've been relocated to a similar planet without realizing it."

"Why would the Federation or the Son'a wish to move the Ba'ku?"

Picard shook his head. "I don't—"

Without warning, phaser fire raked their position. As sparks showered down on them, they ran for cover.

Bolts of plasma ricocheted around the village, destroying buildings, rocks, and sky. Wherever the phasers hit, Picard saw the black and yellow grid of the holodeck underneath.

He grabbed Anij and tried to hurry her toward the hatch, while Data stood his ground and fired back. But they couldn't tell where shots were coming from, or how many enemies were in here. As Anij had asked him, *Who was the enemy?*

In smoke and sparks, the Ba'ku village crumbled all around them. While Data blazed away, Picard and Anij scrambled for their lives.

CHAPTER
6

As phaser fire chewed up the holodeck and the fake Ba'ku village, Picard steered Anij toward the hatch. Dodging the phasers, Data did his best to return fire. But in the confusion and smoke, it was hard to see the enemy.

Picard pushed Anij out of the hatch and he heard a splash. Convinced she was safe, he crouched down and fired in the same direction Data was firing. Finally the shots stopped and, as the smoke cleared, Picard could see that a Son'a officer had tumbled off the roof of a Ba'ku hut and landed in the dust.

"Computer," ordered Picard, panting for breath. "End program and decloak the vessel."

When the holographic image disappeared, they were left standing inside an empty holodeck which took up most of the small spaceship. Data checked the Son'a sniper and found that the fall from the roof had killed him.

"Help!" shouted a voice. "I can't swim!"

Picard and Data climbed out of the hatch to see Anij splashing furiously in the water. The rowboat was floating away from her.

"Don't panic!" ordered the captain.

"I've been shot at," she sputtered, "then thrown from an invisible ship that's come to kidnap us all! Why should I panic?"

"In the event of a water landing," said Data calmly, "I have been designed to serve as a flotation device." The android twisted his neck, plunged into the water, and floated like a log. Anij held on to him gratefully, while Picard swam to retrieve the boat.

On the *Enterprise* a few minutes later, the captain stepped down from the transporter platform. With a shiver, he shook the water off his clothes. When he looked around the transporter room, he saw Worf—with a huge red blemish on his nose.

The captain wanted to look at something else, so he turned to make sure that Data had arrived safely. The wet android gave him a nod, as if everything had returned to normal.

"Commander Worf," said the captain, "did any of the hostages mention a cloaked ship during their debriefings?"

"No, sir," answered the Klingon with surprise.

"Debrief them again." The captain couldn't ignore the blotch on Worf's nose. "Have you been in a fight, Commander?"

The Klingon cringed with embarrassment. "No, sir. It's . . . a gorch."

"Gorch?" asked Picard.

"A pimple," whispered Data, "typical of adolescence."

"Oh, well, it's hardly noticeable," replied the captain, not sounding very convincing.

The captain exited into the corridor, where he ran into Will Riker, looking different somehow. Younger. *Has he lost weight?*

Riker smiled at his puzzled expression and stroked his clean-shaven jaw. He was without a beard for the first time in years. "Smooth as a baby's bottom," bragged Riker.

"I beg your pardon, sir?" asked Data in amazement.

Riker just ignored the android's quizzical stare and reported to the captain, "Admiral Dougherty wants to know why we haven't left yet."

"We're not going anywhere." His jaw set, Picard strode into the turbolift. "Deck five."

Riker turned and looked at Worf. Like everyone else, he was unable to avoid the gorch. "You Klingons never do anything small, do you?"

Worf scowled and stepped toward Picard. "Dr. Crusher asked to talk to you when you returned."

As they exited the turbolift, the captain tapped his combadge. "Picard to Crusher."

"Captain, the Son'a hostages declined to be examined," said the doctor. "I had them confined to quarters."

"And our people?"

"They're fine. In fact, they're better than fine. Increased metabolism, high energy, improved muscle tone. We should all be so lucky."

"Very good, Doctor. Picard out." He turned to his staff. "The Son'a officers are not to be released until I've met with Ru'afo."

"Yes, sir."

Picard headed for his quarters, intending to change. As he walked away, Data touched Riker's clean chin. "Sir," said Data, "it is not as smooth as an *android's* bottom."

Inside his cabin, the captain took a moment to look in the mirror as he unbuttoned his collar. He was shocked to see the skin under his neck—the wrinkles were gone! In their place was smooth, youthful skin.

"Computer," he said, "music."

A Beethoven concerto began to play, but Picard shook his head. "No, not that. Something else . . . something Latin."

"Please specify," asked the computer.

"A mambo!" The rhythmic beat and strumming guitars filled the room. *Much better,* he thought.

After cleaning up and changing into a new uniform, Captain Picard beamed back down to the planet, heading for Anij's simple house. The village was peaceful and dark—with a scent of home cooking on the warm breeze. It felt like a rural town on Earth six hundred years ago.

He rapped on the door and heard voices inside. When Anij answered the door, he had only one question: "How old are you?"

She sighed. "I'll let Sojef tell you."

Picard, Anij, Artim, and Tournel sat around the table and listened as Sojef told the story: "We came here from a solar system where technology had created weapons that threatened to destroy all life. A small group of us set off to find a new home—a home that would be isolated from the threats of other worlds."

He added, "That was three hundred and nine years ago."

"You've not aged a day since then?" asked Picard in shock.

"Actually," replied Sojef, "I was a good deal older when we arrived, in terms of my physical condition."

Anij explained, "There's an unusual metaphasic radiation coming from the planet's rings. It continuously regenerates our genetic structure. You must have noticed the effects by now."

"We've just begun to," said Picard, touching the tight skin under his chin. He looked at the boy, Artim. "I suppose you're seventy-five."

"No, I'm twelve," answered Artim, looking at the captain as if he were crazy.

"The metaphasic radiation won't begin to affect him until he reaches maturity," said Tournel.

Picard gazed at them with a mixture of envy and dread. "To many offlanders, what you have here would be more precious than gold-pressed latinum. I'm afraid it's the reason someone is trying to take this world away from you."

Artim gulped. "The artificial life-form was right."

"If not for Data, you'd probably have been relocated by now," the captain admitted. *And no one would ever know. . . .*

"How can we possibly defend ourselves?" asked Tournel with concern.

"The moment we pick up a weapon," warned Sojef, "we become one of *them.* We lose everything we are—"

"It may not come to that. Clearly, the architects of this conspiracy have tried to keep it a secret. Not just from you, but from my people as well." Picard balled his hand into a fist. "I don't intend to let them."

Later that night, near dawn, Captain Picard took a walk with Anij. They strolled through the peaceful, lantern-lit streets of the village. Anij was wistful and sad.

"We've always known," she told him, "that to survive we had to remain apart. It hasn't been easy. Many of the young people here want to know more about the offland. They're attracted to stories of a faster pace of life."

Picard smiled. "Most of the people who live that faster pace would sell their souls to slow it down."

"But not you?"

"There are days—" he admitted.

"You're not like the others—tempted by the promise of perpetual youth?"

"Who wouldn't be?" answered the captain. "But some of the darkest chapters in the history of my world have involved the forced relocation of a small group of people to satisfy the demands of a larger one. I'd like to believe we learned from our mistakes. Obviously, some of us haven't."

Picard paused to look at a beautiful, handcrafted quilt displayed on a table. The quilt was a work of art, and he was surprised to find it so soft to the touch. "The craftsmanship is extraordinary."

"This is a school, and that's the work of students," she explained. "They're almost ready to become apprentices. In thirty or forty years, some of them will take their place among the artisans."

"Apprenticing for *thirty* years," said Picard, marveling. "We've noticed your people's mental discipline. Did that develop here?"

"Let me ask *you* a question," said Anij. "Have you ever experienced a perfect moment in time?"

"A perfect moment?"

"When time seemed to stop, and you could almost live in that moment."

Picard smiled wistfully. "Yes, seeing my home planet from space for the first time."

"Exactly! And it's nothing more complicated than perception. *You* explore the universe. We've discovered that a single moment in time can be a universe in itself . . . full of powerful forces. Most people aren't aware enough of the *now* to ever notice them."

"I wish I could spare a few centuries to learn," said Picard. As they strolled to her house, Picard smiled at his attractive friend. "There's just one thing I don't understand. In three hundred years, you never learned how to *swim?"*

"I just haven't gotten around to it yet." Anij paused in the doorway and gazed at him. "I wonder if you're aware of the trust you engender, Jean-Luc Picard. In my experience, that's unusual for someone so . . . young. Good night."

"Good night." In this romantic village, feeling forty years younger than he was, Picard wanted to kiss Anij. But she slipped inside her house and was gone before he could.

He kept walking through the quiet streets, until he reached the central courtyard. In a silvery, predawn light, he saw someone in uniform standing in the yard, gazing at the dark horizon. As he drew closer, he saw it was La Forge.

"Geordi!" he called, walking toward him. When the engineer turned around, Picard couldn't help but stare—his implants were gone! For the first time, Picard gazed into Geordi's real eyes.

La Forge beamed with happiness. "Funniest thing, Captain. There wasn't anything wrong with my implants. There was something *right* with my eyes. When Dr. Crusher removed the ocular connections,

A stranger disrupts the Ba'ku village.

Captain Jean-Luc Picard (Patrick Stewart) and the crew of the *U.S.S. Enterprise* NCC-1701-E host the Evoran delegation.

Admiral Dougherty (Anthony Zerbe) and Ru'afo (F. Murray Abraham) plan the evacuation of the Ba'ku homeworld.

Will Riker (Jonathan Frakes) and Deanna Troi (Marina Sirtis) research what little is known about the Son'a and the Ba'ku.

Dr. Beverly Crusher (Gates McFadden) discovers that Geordi La Forge (Levar Burton) no longer needs his implants to see.

Artim (Michael Welch) worries about the strangers in his village.

Captain Picard, Anij (Donna Murphy), Sojef (Daniel Hugh Kelly), and Artim prepare to evacuate the village before the Ba'ku can be transported away.

Artim asks Data (Brent Spinner), "Haven't you ever just played for fun?"

"Take cover!" Worf
(Michael Dorn)
shouts.

"How long can we hold them off?"

"I'm losing her!"

"Red alert! All hands to battle stations!"

"Looking for this?"

"These are perilous times for the Federation. I can't abandon it to people who would threaten everything I've spent a lifetime defending...."

she found that the cells around my optic nerves had regenerated."

He gazed at the horizon, where a glimmer of golden light had begun to creep over the hills. "My sight may not last after we leave this planet. If not, I just wanted to see a sunrise. I've never seen a sunrise, at least, not the way you see them."

A flaming crown of light suddenly burst over the distant hills. Golden sunlight rippled across the lake and the fields, then bathed the tiny village in beauty. Chirping loudly, a flock of birds soared over the village. If there were any more beautiful place in the galaxy, Picard had not seen it.

When he looked at Geordi, he saw tears rolling down the engineer's face.

Four Son'a warships surrounded the *Enterprise* in space. They weren't firing, but their presence was hardly peaceful. In his ready room, Captain Picard kept the *Enterprise* on yellow alert as he prepared to meet his visitors.

A moment later, Admiral Dougherty and Ahdar Ru'afo were conducted into the office. Ru'afo was so angry that the skin on his face looked as tight as a drum. "Am I to understand that you're not releasing my men, Captain?"

Picard looked across his desk at the Son'a commander. "I found the holoship in the lake."

That stopped the sputtering Son'a, who looked to

Dougherty for help. The admiral frowned, realizing that he had better attend to damage control. "Ru'afo, why don't you let the captain and me—"

"No!" yelled Ru'afo. His tight skin began to split in anger. A crack opened from his forehead to his chin, and blood dribbled out of it. "This entire mission has been one Federation blunder after another. You will return my men, or this alliance will end with the *destruction* of your ship!" Dabbing at his bloody face, Ru'afo strode out of the ready room.

Dougherty sighed. "You're looking well, Jean-Luc. Rested."

"Your Briar Patch turned out to be more hospitable than I expected," answered Picard.

"That's why we put chromodynamic shields in place, so our people wouldn't feel the effects from the metaphasic radiation."

"Or understand that they were participating in the outright *theft* of a world. I won't let you move them, Admiral. I'll go to the Federation Council."

"I'm acting on *orders* from the Federation Council," answered Dougherty.

"How can there be an order to abandon the Prime Directive?"

The admiral paced the small office. "The Prime Directive doesn't apply. These people are not native to this world. They were never meant to be immortal. We'll simply be restoring their natural evolution."

Picard stared at him, aghast. "Who are *we* to decide the next course of evolution for these people?"

"There are *six hundred* people down there. We'll be able to use the regenerative properties of this radiation to help *billions*. The Son'a have developed a procedure to collect the metaphasic particles from the planet's rings. They're our partners."

"Our partners are nothing more than petty thugs," countered Picard.

"With metaphasics," said Dougherty, "life spans will be doubled. An entirely new medical science will evolve. I understand your chief engineer has the use of his eyes for the first time in his life. Would you take his sight away from him?"

"There are metaphasic particles all over the Briar Patch. Why must this planet be—"

"Because of the concentration in the rings," cut in Dougherty. "To collect the radiation, the Son'a have a process which starts a thermolytic reaction. After it's over, the planet will be unlivable for generations."

Picard shook his head, still disgusted with the plan. "Delay the procedure. Let my people look at the technology."

"Our best scientific minds already have—we can't find another way."

"Can't the Son'a establish a separate colony on this planet until we find—"

"No," answered the admiral. "For the Son'a, it would take ten years of regular exposure to reverse the condition. Some of them won't survive that long. Besides, they don't want to live in the middle of the Briar Patch. Who would?"

"The Ba'ku," said Picard grimly. "We are betraying the principles upon which the Federation was *founded*. This is an attack on the very soul of the Federation, and it will destroy the Ba'ku."

The admiral walked to the door. "I'm ordering you to the Goren system. File whatever protests you want. By the time you do, the operation will be over. I'm also ordering the release of the Son'a officers."

The admiral stalked out of the ready room. The captain had his orders, and he knew what he had to do.

"Picard to bridge," he said. "Prepare the ship for departure at oh-seven-hundred hours."

CHAPTER 7

Subahdar Gallatin strode from the transporter room into the Body Enhancement Center on the Son'a ship. He found his commander, Ru'afo, undergoing laser repair on his face. A beautiful attendant carefully stretched his face and repaired the cracks, but the ahdar still looked older.

"Gallatin!" said Ru'afo with delight. "So the righteous Starfleet captain finally released you. Did you encounter any problems on the surface?"

"No, sir. But it wasn't easy, being among them."

"I'm sure," replied Ru'afo disdainfully. "Just don't forget what they did to us. We'll have them rounded up in a day or two. We needn't bother with the Federation holoship anymore. Just get the holding cells ready."

"Yes, sir," replied Gallatin. *I wish there was some other way. . . .*

Ru'afo touched his female attendant's skilled hands and said, "I'm going to miss these little flesh-stretching sessions of ours, my dear."

Picard fastened the top button of his shirt, noting the absence of the four captain's pips which usually graced his collar. Now the pips lay in his dresser, along with his uniform. He was wearing civilian clothes.

Heading for the hangar bay, the captain settled into the cockpit of the captain's yacht and studied a large image of the planet. *There's room for so many people on three lush continents—why do the Son'a have to take everything?*

As he was plotting his course, the hatch opened behind him. The captain turned to see Data, Riker, Troi, Crusher, La Forge, and Worf file onto the ship. Only Riker and La Forge were wearing their uniforms. The others looked as if they were dressed for a trip.

"Taking the captain's yacht out for a spin?" asked Deanna, a twinkle in her eye.

Worf glanced at the storage units Picard had piled in the back of the yacht. "Seven metric tons of ultritium explosives, eight tetryon pulse launchers, ten isomagnetic disintegrators—"

"You must be planning on doing some hunting," said Riker.

"Go back to your quarters," ordered the captain, rising to his feet. "That's an order."

No one moved, and Riker observed, "No uniform, no orders."

Geordi La Forge looked at the captain with his vibrant brown eyes. "How could I look at another sunrise, knowing what my sight cost these people?"

Data said, "I feel obliged to point out that the environmental anomalies may be stimulating certain rebellious instincts common to youth. That could affect everyone's judgment, except mine of course."

"Okay, Data, what do you think we should do?" asked Beverly.

The android paused for a fraction of a second to think about it. "Saddle up, lock and load."

"They won't begin the procedure while the planet is inhabited," the captain explained. "So our job is to keep the planet *inhabited.*"

He looked at Riker and La Forge, knowing they would have a tough time, too. "Go back and put a face on what's happening here. Make the Council *see* the Ba'ku. It's too easy to turn a blind eye to the suffering of an unfamiliar people."

Picard looked more sharply at Riker. "We'll hold out as long as we can."

The ahdar was in such a good mood lately that Gallatin hated to spoil it. They had all thought the last obstacle was gone, but perhaps that wasn't so.

Gallatin entered the tactical room while the ahdar

was running a computer simulation. In vivid animation, the injector assembly fired a charge into the planet's rings. It started a thermolytic reaction which consumed the planet.

"The injector performs perfectly in every simulation," bragged Ru'afo.

Gallatin said, "Sir, as the *Enterprise* left orbit, one of their support craft went down to the surface. It appeared to be the captain's yacht. Five persons were on board." He handed Ru'afo a padd containing this information.

The ahdar scowled, careful not to split his face. "We're not waiting until morning. Take the shuttles and get everyone off the surface tonight. If Picard or any of his people interfere, *eliminate* them."

As the bells sounded an urgent peal, the Ba'ku villagers rushed from their homes. Leaders stood in the streets, directing them into lines and trying to answer questions.

"We're leaving the village," Tournel explained to a frightened family. "Take only what you need—and food. We may not be back for days."

"No, there's no time to take furniture!" Anij told two men carrying a bed. "But bring the blankets."

Animals also crammed the dusty streets, many of them laden with their owners' belongings. Picard stood in the middle of the bedlam, studying his maps. They had to hide—not just from scanners and eyes, but from transporters.

Data cut through the crowd and stopped to report, "Captain, I've activated transport inhibitors around the village."

"Good." Picard motioned to Sojef and Anij to join them, and he showed them his charts. "There are veins of kelbonite running through the hills. The more concentrated the deposits, the more trouble they'll have with their transporters.

"Our route will keep us as close to these deposits as possible. When we're forced away from the terrain, we'll use transport inhibitors. The mountains have the highest concentrations. Once we're there, transport will be virtually impossible."

"There are caves in those mountains," said Anij.

The captain nodded confidently. "We can hold them off a long time . . . once we get there."

Artim was scared as he ran beside his father through the freshly planted fields. All around them it was panic, with people falling down, dropping their things. The boy reached down to pick up a jewelry box for a little girl, and his father pulled him away.

"Don't try to carry too much," Sojef warned the children. "We've got a long climb ahead of us, and—"

Before he could finish, the ground shuddered, and horrible booms pounded in their ears. As a fleet of Son'a shuttlecraft streaked over their heads, the people screamed and shouted. More explosions ripped the countryside, and Artim and Sojef were bumped by people running in every direction.

Artim saw the big offlander with the deep voice—the Klingon. He was striding through the crowd, trying to reach the captain. "We've lost an inhibitor!" he yelled. "There's a gap in the field."

Suddenly, people around Artim began to *disappear*. One moment they were there, then came a sparkle of light, and they were gone! A panicked man bumped into the boy and knocked him to the ground.

In the stampede of people, a careless foot kicked the boy. When more people disappeared, the panic got worse, and Artim couldn't find his father.

The frightened people turned into a mob. They pushed him to the ground and trampled him! Suddenly, strong arms lifted him out of the crush. Artim looked up, expecting to see his father—but it was the artificial man!

Data said, "Your father has been transported to a spaceship. He has not been harmed."

Captain Picard tried to calm the panicked people. "Stay in the protected areas! We'll be safe until we get into the hills."

Artim wondered if they would ever be safe again.

Admiral Dougherty tried to gulp down the knot in his throat. But it stuck like a rock in his stomach. He knew what he had to do, because his whole career was wrapped up in this operation. Not only that, but metaphasics was the future of the Federation.

No longer would they be weak, at constant war with

other powers in the quadrant. They would be immortal!

"The *Enterprise* is only nineteen hours from communications range with the Federation," said Ru'afo worriedly.

"I'll order Riker to turn around," answered Dougherty.

"Picard's first officer?" said Ru'afo. "Do you really believe he'll listen? You can't let him get back and delay this operation. After it's done and everyone receives the benefits, we'll all be heroes."

The Son'a pointed at his viewscreen. "My ships are capable of intercepting the *Enterprise* before it reaches the perimeter. I could send them to . . . *escort* it back. But Commander Riker might not want to come . . ." He trailed off.

If it comes down to force . . . Dougherty nodded. "Send your ships."

In the steep foothills, a long line of people and animals snaked along a narrow trail. Artim could barely see the Ba'ku village far in the distance. He could see Captain Picard and Anij leading the way. Data walked beside him. The boy kept looking for his father, finding it hard to believe that he was gone.

He glanced up and saw Data looking at him. "My father told me I shouldn't talk to you."

"I understand," replied the android.

"I don't," admitted the boy. "Not everyone agrees

with him, you know, about machines. There was even a big fight about it once. Do you like being a machine?"

"I aspire to be more than I am," answered Data.

"I know why," said Artim with a smile. "So people like us won't be afraid of you anymore."

"Perhaps."

Artim trudged along, getting very tired. "Don't you ever get tired?"

"My power cells continually recharge themselves."

The boy shook his head. "I can't imagine what it would be like to be a machine."

They talked about the differences between biological and mechanical beings, between adults and children. It became clear that Data envied people, and wanted to be like them.

Artim set him straight. "But you've never had adults telling you what to do all the time. Or bedtime, or having to eat foods you don't like."

"I would gladly accept the requirement of a bedtime in exchange for knowing what it is like to be a child," admitted Data.

"Do machines ever play?"

"I play the violin," answered Data. "And my chess routines are quite advanced."

"No, I mean, haven't you ever just *played* for fun?"

"Androids don't have fun."

"Why not?"

The android cocked his head. "No one's ever asked me that before."

"Well," said the boy, "if you want to know what it's like to be a child, you need to learn how to play."

As they climbed the path, the boy looked up at the head of the trail. He saw Captain Picard walking very close to Anij, their hands almost touching. They looked at each other with fondness and respect. The Ba'ku had lost so much, including his father—but maybe Anij had found something.

On the bridge of the *Enterprise,* Riker sat in the command chair. Impatiently, he drummed his fingers on the arm of the chair while he watched the bridge crew at work. Perim was on the conn, La Forge on ops, and Nara at tactical. It seemed to be taking forever to get out of the Briar Patch.

"Commander," said Perim. "I'm showing two Son'a ships on an intercept course."

Uh-oh . . . "How long till they reach us?" asked Riker.

"Eighteen minutes," answered Perim.

Geordi shook his head. "We're not going to be able to get a transmission out of here for at least another hour."

"They're hailing us," reported Nara.

"Tell them our receiver assembly is down," replied Riker. "That we can send messages but not receive."

Nara worked his controls. "I don't think they believe us."

"Why not?"

The ship was jolted by a sudden impact, and the

acting captain looked at his readouts. "A photon torpedo. Isn't that the universal greeting when communications are down?"

"I think it's the universal greeting when you don't like someone," said Geordi.

Another torpedo shook them slightly, and Riker ordered, "Full impulse."

"The manifolds can't handle full impulse in the Patch," reported La Forge.

"If we don't outrun them, the manifolds are going to be the only thing left of this ship."

"I'll be in engineering," said La Forge. He rose from his station, and a relief officer took his place.

"Red alert!" announced Riker to his shipmates. "All hands, battle stations!"

CHAPTER
8

Two Son'a warships chased the *Enterprise* through the swirling Briar Patch, firing at will. Her rear shields sparkled under the phaser blasts, weakening with every strike. The *Enterprise* returned fire, but she couldn't stop both of them. She was forced to zig and zag, which was difficult in the thick clouds of the Briar Patch.

On the bridge, smoke was everywhere, and sparks sputtered from burned-out consoles. Relief crew members rushed to replace injured officers, and security tried to douse the fires. Nara's voice cut through the bedlam, "Shields at sixty percent!"

"Acknowledged," said Riker in the command chair.

From engineering, Geordi reported, "Commander,

we're burning deuterium down here! We're going to blow *ourselves* up—we won't need any help from the Son'a!"

Riker walked to the conn and pointed to a huge nebula off the starboard. "What's inside that nebula cluster?" he asked Perim.

"Cometary debris, pockets of unstable metreon gas. We don't want to go in there, sir."

"Yes, we do." He tapped Perim on the shoulder. "You're relieved, Ensign. Take over at ops."

Riker took control of the conn and said to himself, "Time to use the Briar Patch like Br'er Rabbit did—"

With the commander at the helm, they dodged the Son'a ships long enough to reach the stellar debris of the nebula. The cobwebs of primal matter exploded when the Son'a torpedoes struck. This started a chain reaction which rippled through subspace. Like a brilliant wave, the burst of light cascaded toward the *Enterprise.*

Nara shouted, "Sir! They've detonated an isolytic burst! A subspace tear is forming."

"On screen," ordered Riker.

The bridge crew watched in horror as the subspace ripple chased them through the nebula. "I thought subspace weapons were banned by the Khitomer Accord," said Ensign Perim.

"Remind me to lodge a protest," muttered Riker.

Geordi's voice broke over the comm panel. "Commander, our warp coil is acting like a magnet to the tear. We're pulling it like a zipper across space!"

"Options?" asked Riker.

"Eject the core."

"Will that stop the tear?"

"You've got me, Commander."

"That's your expert opinion?" snapped Riker, looking at the anomaly surging after them.

"Detonating the warp core might neutralize the cascade," answered Geordi, "but then again, it might not. Subspace weapons are unpredictable—*that's* why they were banned."

"The tear is closing on us," reported Nara. "Impact in fifteen seconds!"

"Eject the core!" ordered Riker.

"I just did," came Geordi's hoarse reply.

"Impact in ten seconds," Nara said nervously.

"Detonate!" ordered Riker.

In the middle of the dense nebula, the ejected warp core exploded violently. A cloud of gas and debris rushed outward, devouring everything in its path. The *Enterprise* was buffeted by the shock wave.

On the bridge, consoles exploded, and crew members were knocked off their feet. Security rushed to put out more fires, as medical staff hurried to tend the wounded. Riker picked himself up off the deck and shook his head. *This is like the worst of the Dominion War,* he thought. *Or the Borg . . .*

"It worked!" announced Nara in amazement. "The tear has been sealed."

La Forge reported, "There's nothing to stop them

from doing it again. And we're fresh out of warp coils."

"We're still thirty-six minutes from transmission range, sir," said Perim on ops.

Riker grit his teeth. "We're through running from them."

On the planet, Picard, Anij, and the rest of the Ba'ku villagers stopped to rest on the steep trail. Despite climbing all day and running from enemy fire, the captain felt full of energy. He could tell there had been a dramatic improvement in his stamina and strength.

He glanced at Deanna, Beverly, Worf, and his other old comrades. They also looked healthier, younger, and more fit. Worf's hair seemed to have grown ten centimeters and was sticking out wildly. Beverly and Deanna giggled like teenagers over something.

Suddenly the captain heard rocket thrusters, and he looked up to see a fleet of Son'a shuttlecraft headed toward them. The Ba'ku ran for cover, but the shuttlecraft stayed high in the sky. As they flew over, they released dozens of small drones, no bigger than footballs.

Like a flock of robotic birds, the drones spread out and came after them. Picard could see them blinking, scanning, looking for warm bodies.

"Take cover!" shouted Worf.

But it was too late—the drones were already zooming toward them. Data, Worf, and Picard aimed phasers and fired at the approaching craft, but they were too small and swift to make good targets. Data managed to destroy two of them, but dozens more kept coming.

As it passed by, one of the drones shot a small dart. The dart hit a Ba'ku woman in the back, and she slumped to the ground. When Picard moved to help her, she disappeared in a column of sparkling lights. She had been *transported!* The same thing happened to several more Ba'ku.

"Isolinear tags!" said Worf, yelling above the panic. "Their transporters can lock on to them."

"We have to find shelter," ordered Picard.

Anij grabbed his arm and pointed. "There's a cavern at the base of the next hill."

"This way!" shouted the captain, waving his arm to the frightened Ba'ku.

The refugees overcame their panic long enough to follow him. With the help of Anij and his crew, they herded the people and their animals into the narrow mouth of the cave. They tramped through hot, muddy springs, ignoring the steam and rotten smells. Picard looked worriedly down the trail, where he could see others still in danger.

"Hurry!" he shouted.

On the path, Artim tried to keep up with Data, but it was hard with so many frightened people. The android stopped to fire at the drones chasing them, and his aim was deadly. He shot down four of them, but more kept coming. Whenever they hit someone with their darts, that person disappeared a few seconds later.

They've joined my father, thought Artim. He was worried for them, but he was glad his father wouldn't be alone.

When the boy scrambled over a ridge, he saw something terrible—three of the enemy! They were chasing the villagers, trying to capture them. "Data!" yelled Artim.

The android was instantly at his side. Just as quickly, Data decided what he should do. With an amazing leap, he grabbed one of the Son'a drones and aimed it at the enemy soldiers. Before they could react, it shot them with darts. A moment later they disappeared along with the others.

Satisfied, Data lifted the Son'a drone and crushed it between his powerful hands. Then he aimed his phaser and kept shooting, allowing Artim and the others to reach the safety of the cave.

The boy missed his father, but he was glad to have Data as a friend. He touched his pocket and felt a slight squirming. Despite everything, his palm pet was okay, too.

With Picard and Anij leading the way, the Ba'ku refugees found their way to the center of the cavern. Everywhere was mud, steam, bubbling hot springs, and water dripping from the ceiling. It reminded Picard of a Swedish sauna.

The exhausted people and their frightened animals tried to find someplace to rest in the damp cave. A lot of them collapsed into the mud, just glad to be alive. He could tell from their faces that they had never been through anything like this, even though they were hundreds of years old.

The captain looked back at the mouth of the cavern, and he saw Worf turning on a forcefield. *We're safe, but for how long?*

Data walked up to him, and Picard sighed. "How many?"

"Another forty-three people reported taken, sir," answered the android.

The captain frowned, wondering if they could have kept those people safe. He tried not to be too hard on himself. After all, they had moved as quickly as they could, and there was nowhere else to go.

Without warning, the ground shook, and an explosion echoed in the vast cavern. Dust tumbled down from the fragile ceiling, and everyone looked up. Boom! Boom! Boom!—the explosions kept pounding the mountain above them.

Worf strode to his side, and the Klingon looked grim. "They're trying to force us out, so their drones can tag us."

Picard turned to Data, who was working his tricorder. The android reported, "With all the hydrothermal vents in the substrata, the structural integrity of this cavern is not going to hold for long."

The forcefield flickered as half a dozen drones tried

to get in. "Is there another way out of here?" the captain asked Anij.

The Ba'ku woman shook her head. For the first time, she looked frightened and hopeless.

Data began to follow a stream of steamy water. "Tracking the water flow may reveal another potential exit."

Now Worf, Crusher, and Troi checked their tricorders, trying to help the android find a way out. The bombardment continued above their heads, filling the cavern with dust, noise, and panic.

Data approached a damp cave wall and felt the lime deposits crusted on the rock. Water disappeared into a crevice at his feet. "I'm showing a nitrogen-oxygen flow behind this calcite formation, Captain."

"Will the roof hold if we blast through?" asked Picard.

"I believe it is safe, sir."

Picard drew his phaser, and so did the others. Taking careful aim, they blasted the wall. A few moments later they had a hole large enough to crawl through to the chamber beyond. The captain could smell fresh, cool air.

He motioned to his comrades. "Spread out as far as you can. Get everyone into those caves, and set up forcefields once you're inside."

At once, his loyal staff began to round up the Ba'ku. *We aren't beaten yet,* decided the captain.

* * *

On the bridge of the *Enterprise,* Riker tried to ignore the blood on his face and his banged-up arm. He stared grimly at the viewscreen, watching the dust of dead suns swirl around them. There were also pockets of gas, and something looked familiar about them.

He tapped his comm panel. "Geordi, are those pockets of metreon gas?"

"Aye, sir," answered La Forge's voice. "Highly volatile—I recommend we keep our distance."

"Negative," answered Riker. "I want to use the ramscoop to collect as much of it as we can."

"The purpose being?" asked La Forge.

Riker pounded a fist on his chair. "The purpose being, I intend to *ram* it down their throat."

Ensign Nara cleared his throat. "Commander, if one of their weapons hits that gas—"

Geordi broke in. "I wouldn't be surprised if history remembers this as the Riker Maneuver."

"If it *works,* you mean," added the acting captain.

"Even if it doesn't," said Geordi, "they'll be teaching kids at the Academy *not* to do this for years."

"Activate ramscoop," ordered Riker.

On the outer hull of the *Enterprise,* hatches pulled back to reveal the scoop. Gas clouds swirled into it, being compressed and processed as they were absorbed. Deep in the ship, storage tanks filled with the metreon.

La Forge strained to read all the displays and

complained, "How do you people get anything done with such limited eyes? I'm ready to get my implants back." A few seconds later he reported, "Storage cells are at maximum capacity—five thousand cubic meters of metreon gas."

"Stand by," said Riker, sitting stiffly at the conn. "Computer, access manual steering column."

At once a molded joystick popped out of the console. Riker grabbed the stick, a determined look on his face. "Transfer helm control to manual."

He put the joystick forward, speeding through the eerie dust clouds of the nebula. The Son'a ships lay dead ahead in the clearing. He could see them, waiting like vultures. The *Enterprise* zoomed out of the nebula and closed fast on the enemy.

"They're powering their forward weapons array!" warned Perim.

"Blow out the ramscoop!" ordered Riker. "Stand by full thrusters."

"Ramscoop released!" echoed Geordi's voice.

Riker yanked the joystick and put the *Enterprise* into a sharp turn—just as the Son'a ships fired. Their beams hit the concentrated gases, and the fabric of space erupted. A ripple of fire engulfed both Son'a ships, and one exploded immediately. The other careered into space, burning out of control.

With the shock wave chasing them, Riker didn't wait to see any more. He didn't relax his hand on the controls until they were far from the inferno. Then he looked back with grim satisfaction. *The Son'a are overconfident,* he decided, *and that could be their greatest weakness.*

Picard, Worf, Crusher, Data, and Troi crawled out of the cave and found themselves in a mountain pass. The captain realized they would have to dash across the open before they could get to another underground cave. Shuttlecraft continued blasting the hills, but at a distance. *Maybe the Son'a have lost track of them,* thought Picard hopefully.

Suddenly the ground in front of them was chewed up by phaser fire, and they scrambled for cover. Worf pointed to a nearby hill. "Up there!"

Picard raised his head and could see a team of three on the planet surface; they were led by a Son'a officer. "Data, Troi, keep these people moving," he ordered. "Worf, Crusher—with me!"

Crouching behind a boulder, Picard fired at the enemy, giving his comrades cover. Worf hefted a large weapon—an isometric disintegrator—and took aim. He blasted a shot, and the weapon roared like a handheld rocket launcher.

The hill blew up in a cloud of dust and debris. The Son'a officer rolled through the thickets and came to rest not far from them. Picard made sure there were no more enemy in the area; then he motioned Crusher toward the body.

Dr. Crusher knelt down and studied the fallen Son'a with her tricorder. The captain could tell from her expression that something was wrong.

"Will he live?" asked the captain.

"Yes. But look at this medscan." Beverly handed him her tricorder, and the captain studied the read-outs.

He could hardly believe the results. "How could this be possible?"

Crusher shook her head. "Maybe we should ask them."

Artim hung back with the last group of Ba'ku waiting to leave the cavern. They needed someone to guide them through the twisty tunnels. He could hear the Son'a shuttlecraft pounding the hillside overhead, and he didn't want to go out there.

It was dusty and steamy inside the cavern, but it felt safer to be underground. As long as he had his little pet to keep him company. The boy looked in his pocket to make sure his tentacled pet was safe—but he couldn't find it! He patted down his clothing, but it was *gone*.

As Artim crawled through the mud, searching for his pet, Anij and Tournel entered the cavern. The others jumped up, eager to go, but Artim crawled deeper into the cave. He couldn't leave until he found his pet!

Behind him, he heard voices:

"Is that everyone?" asked Anij.

"The boy!" shouted someone.

Artim crawled faster, because he didn't want to be

forced to leave without his only belonging. He reached into a puddle and scalded his hands in the steaming water. That wouldn't work, so he tried to remember all the places he had been.

Yes! The rock where I ate lunch.

Artim jumped to his feet and ran to the dry boulder where he had sat down to eat some dried fruit and muffins. Once again, he slithered through the mud, looking for his precious pet. Finally he saw it, crawling slowly toward him, like a caterpillar with eight heads.

Just as Artim's hand engulfed his pet, two strong hands grabbed him.

Anij yanked him off the ground and set him on his feet. "Artim! What are you doing?"

He gulped at her and stuffed his pet into his pocket. As explosions rocked the cavern and dirt crumbled down on them, Anij grabbed his hand and ran for it.

Now it seemed as if every Son'a ship was firing at the hillside over their heads. In the smoke and debris, Artim couldn't even see the mouth of the cave.

"Anij!" called Tournel in the distance.

"I've got him!" she shouted back. When the boy fell behind, Anij gave him a good pull.

They could see vague figures in the distance—Picard, Tournel, Worf, and others. Artim rubbed the dirt out of his eyes—he could barely see! He blinked and saw somebody moving toward them—Captain Picard.

Just as they reached the mouth of the cave, an explosion struck right over their heads. The ceiling made a terrible rumble, then it began to collapse! Picard grabbed Artim and threw him out of the cave, but tons of rocks and dirt fell on top of Anij and Picard.

"Anij!" screamed the boy.

CHAPTER 9

Data caught Artim outside the mouth of the cave and pulled him away from the tons of collapsing rock. "Anij!" yelled the boy, fighting against the android. But Data held him tightly, shielding him from the falling rock.

When the dust cleared, the mouth of the cave was completely blocked. Worf, Crusher, and Troi rushed forward to check how bad it was, while Data handed Artim to a waiting Ba'ku.

"Tournel will take you the rest of the way," explained the android.

"No! I want to stay with you!" the boy insisted tearfully.

After what Artim had been through, Data could

forgive his burst of emotion. "It is safer there. I will join you shortly."

Artim reluctantly went with Tournel, and that was one less concern for the android. As Data moved toward the cave-in, he heard Worf trying to raise the captain on his combadge. "Worf to Picard!" shouted the Klingon.

Dr. Crusher studied her medical tricorder. "Two life signs—one extremely faint."

"There are almost four metric tons of rock blocking our way," said Troi glumly as she studied her tricorder. She jumped up and aimed a phaser at the rock pile, but Worf stopped her.

"That might cause another cave-in," warned the Klingon. He immediately began to pull the rocks off the pile with his bare hands.

The Klingon worked frantically, grunting like an animal as he hurled the rocks behind them. Soon Troi, Crusher, and Data pitched in, trying to clear the mouth of the cave. Despite their best efforts, Data doubted they would reach Anij and the captain in time.

Picard coughed the dust out of his lungs and shook off a pounding headache. He touched a damp spot on his face and could feel the blood, but he couldn't see much. Their lamps had gotten crushed in the cave-in, and the only light came from outside—a hole in the ceiling of the cave.

"Anij!" he called. Picard felt around in the rubble

and darkness for the Ba'ku woman but couldn't find her.

His combadge suddenly chirped. "Worf to Picard."

"Yes, yes," he rasped. "I can hear you—"

"We're trying to get to you, sir," reported the Klingon.

The captain's mind was not on them, but on Anij, who was still missing. He crawled through the debris, groping in the darkness. Finally he came to her still body. "Anij!"

Weakly, she opened her eyes and winced in pain. He touched her cheek, then looked to see if he had his tricorder on his belt. *Yes!* He could find out how badly she was hurt.

Picard turned on his tricorder and sat in the dark, studying the readouts. It wasn't good. "Help is coming," he told her.

Anij tried to smile, but she hardly had enough strength for that small gesture. She closed her eyes, and Picard didn't need the tricorder to know that she was slipping away.

"Worf! You must hurry!" he barked into his combadge.

"We're coming as fast as we can," answered the Klingon. "We can't risk using phasers."

"I understand. Tell Dr. Crusher to have a hypospray of lectrazine ready."

Crusher broke in. "How bad is she, Captain?"

He glanced at his tricorder. "I'm losing her."

"We're coming," she assured him.

The captain took her hand and touched it to his cheek. "Stay with me. Don't let go of this moment, Anij. Help me find the power to make you live in this moment. Just one more moment, and then one more after that, and one more after that."

With effort, she opened her eyes, too weak to do anything else. They gazed at each other, and he knew they were connecting. Picard gripped her hand tighter, and he could feel his consciousness merging into her fingers, flowing down her arm.

All of his senses felt alive and vivid; he was seeing with new eyes—*her* eyes. The cave lit up around them, not with real light but with the combined force of their wills. It was almost like a Vulcan mind-meld—two becoming one. Picard felt weaker, but he knew Anij was gaining strength.

Finally she smiled at him, and the cavern seemed to swirl around them. A beam of light broke into their reverie, but it was from behind them. Rocks tumbled away, and Beverly Crusher crawled through, letting in more light.

The doctor quickly applied a hypospray to Anij's neck. The captain sat back and waited nervously as Crusher checked Anij with her medical tricorder. At long last, the doctor looked at the captain and smiled. "She's stabilizing."

"Is it safe to move her?"

"Safer than leaving her in here," answered Beverly.

Picard knelt down and gently picked her up in his arms. Anij looked at him gratefully and said weakly, "You thought it would take centuries to learn."

The captain smiled with affection at the injured woman and carefully carried her through the rubble. He could see the light of the exit just ahead.

A few moments later they emerged into the sunlight. Troi, Worf, and Data looked at them with relief, but there wasn't time for greetings. Five Son'a drones had spotted them and were heading their way.

The captain set Anij on the ground and crouched protectively in front of her. Worf, Troi, Data, and Crusher fanned out around them, drawing their phasers. Worf tossed a phaser rifle to Picard.

It was a showdown. The *Enterprise* crew blazed away as the drones zoomed toward them. When they shot their darts, the Starfleet officers ducked and rolled, and came up firing. Worf blasted one drone, and Data got another. Picard and Crusher combined their fire to destroy a third, and Troi drilled a fourth one.

One more kept coming, kept firing—at the only one who wasn't moving.

With horror, Picard saw the tag hit Anij on the shoulder. When he reached to tear it out, he felt the sting of a dart hitting him in the side. He tried to remove it, but he could already feel the tingle of the transporter beam. Helpless, Picard and Anij disappeared in a sparkling swirl of lights.

* * *

Picard looked around the Son'a brig, which was filled with Ba'ku refugees. It made the *Enterprise*'s brig look like a hotel. At least he could stay close to Anij, who was still very weak and badly injured. It was also good to see Sojef again. None of them said much to each other. What could they say?

He heard a crackling sound, and he turned to see the forcefield on the entrance turn off. Followed by guards, Admiral Dougherty and Subahdar Gallatin entered the brig. They marched straight toward Picard and Anij.

Picard gazed at the admiral, not hiding his distrust of a fellow officer.

"Order them to surrender, and I promise you won't be court-martialed," said Dougherty.

Picard shook his head. "If a court-martial is the only way to tell the people of the Federation what happened here, then I welcome it."

Before they could argue, Ahdar Ru'afo entered the brig and strode toward them, looking angry. He waved a padd in Dougherty's face. "The *Enterprise* has destroyed one of my ships. The other is on fire, requesting assistance."

Picard ignored him and looked at Dougherty. "The *Enterprise* would only fire if it were defending itself. Ru'afo must have ordered an attack. I can't believe he would have given that order without your consent, Admiral." He paused, letting that sink in. "I wonder which one of us will be facing that court-martial?"

Dougherty couldn't meet his eyes. The admiral turned to the Son'a. "There's nothing further to be gained from this."

"You're right," agreed Ru'afo with an edge to his voice. "This is going to end now. The Ba'ku want to stay on the planet? Let them. I'm going to launch the injector."

The admiral scowled and glanced at Picard. For the first time, the captain had a feeling that the admiral might be on his side. "You're not going to launch anything until—"

"In six hours," vowed Ru'afo, "every living thing in this system will be dead, or dying."

The ahdar turned and stalked off, but Picard shouted after him, "You would kill your own people? Your own parents, your brothers, sisters—" Ru'afo froze in midstep.

Dougherty stared at the captain in shock.

"Didn't you know, Admiral?" Picard asked. "The Ba'ku and the Son'a are the same race."

Dougherty looked at Ru'afo, but he didn't turn around.

Sojef, who had been listening, walked up to Ru'afo. "Which one were you? Gal'na? Ro'tin? Belath'nin? I'm sorry, I don't recognize you."

Softly, the Son'a answered, "Those names, those children are gone forever."

"What is he talking about?" demanded Dougherty.

Sojef explained, "A century ago a group of our

young people wanted to follow the ways of the off-landers. They tried to take over the colony, and when they failed—"

"When we failed," hissed Ru'afo, "you *exiled* us. To die slowly."

Picard was surprised when Anij stirred in his arms and sat up. "You're Ro'tin, aren't you? There's something in the voice."

She looked at Gallatin. "Would you be his friend, Gal'na? I helped your mother bathe you when you were a child. She still speaks of you."

Picard fixed Dougherty with an accusing stare. "You've brought the Federation into the middle of a blood feud, Admiral. The children have returned to expel their elders, just as they were once expelled. Except Ru'afo's need for revenge has now escalated to parricide."

Ru'afo stalked out of the brig. Gallatin looked at the Ba'ku in the brig, indecision on his face. Finally he followed his superior out the door.

Dougherty shook his head in disbelief. "It was for the Federation. It was all for the Federation. . . ." He turned and rushed out of the room.

Elloran guards restored the forcefield and took up their positions. *It's up to Dougherty,* thought Picard. *Perhaps he can make them listen.*

His anger growing, Admiral Dougherty searched for Ru'afo until he found the ahdar in the sculpture chamber. This was a part of the Body Enhancement

Facility he had never seen before. All of this equipment, which had looked so wonderful, now looked like a torture chamber. *No wonder they appear so much different from their parents. They do all this to stop the effects of aging. They lost the benefits of the metaphasic radiation when they left the Ba'ku. . . .*

Ru'afo was attached to a machine which bombarded his face with pulsating green energy. He looked as if he were trying to relax, but his fists kept clenching and unclenching.

Dougherty squared his shoulders and said, "We're taking this ship out of here. This mission is over."

"It is *not* over!" declared Ru'afo.

"It is over."

Without warning, Ru'afo jumped up and grabbed Dougherty. He forced the admiral across the room, shouting, "I do not take orders from you!"

Dougherty struggled, but the Son'a was much stronger than he was. "If you begin the procedure while the planet is still populated, the Federation will pursue you until—"

Ru'afo threw the admiral into a treatment chair and locked his head into a face-stretching device. "The Federation," he scoffed, "will never know what happened here."

The admiral struggled, but his head was held tightly. Ru'afo hit the switches on the device—it hummed ominously, and lights began to pulse.

Dougherty screamed as the machine grabbed his ears and began to stretch his face. But he lacked the elasticity of the Son'a skin. Ru'afo held him down—until the admiral's own skin strangled him to death.

Subahdar Gallatin stood on the bridge of the Son'a ship. He glanced at the Tarlac and Elloran crew members, wondering if they knew, or cared, about what their leader was doing. No, they were just mercenaries—paid to obey orders. This was really between the Son'a and the Ba'ku.

The door opened, and Ru'afo strolled onto the bridge. "Admiral Dougherty will not be joining us for dinner," he casually told Gallatin. "Deploy the collector."

When Gallatin hesitated, Ru'afo snapped, "Do you have a problem with those orders?"

"May I talk to you alone?" asked Gallatin.

Ru'afo turned to another Son'a officer. "Deploy the collector." The officer worked his console while Ru'afo moved over to his second-in-command.

"Moving them is one thing," said Gallatin quietly, "killing them all—"

Ru'afo looked puzzledly at him. "No one hated them more than you, Gal'na. We've come a long way together. This is the moment we've planned for so many years."

Gallatin looked at his friend, his commander. *Ru'afo is right.* They had been through so much together. *How can I go against him?*

Ru'afo gave him a friendly pat on the shoulder.

"Separate the Starfleet personnel and secure them in the aft cargo hold. See that Picard joins them."

Gallatin frowned. "The shields in that section won't protect them against the thermolytic reaction."

"Thank you for reminding me."

Ru'afo sat in the captain's chair and watched the collider vessel on the viewscreen. A hatch opened, and the huge sails of the collector slowly extended into space. While the thermolytic reaction consumed the planet and its rings, the collector would capture the metaphasic radiation.

Gallatin realized that in a matter of hours, everything would be dead on his home planet.

CHAPTER

10

Two prisoners in the Son'a brig hoisted Captain Picard up the wall to study the forcefield generators. If he found a way to turn them off, they could escape from the brig and take over the ship. They had enough people.

"Jean-Luc," warned Anij.

The captain jumped to the deck just as Gallatin entered the brig. He aimed a handheld weapon at the captain and said, "Follow me."

Picard gave a reassuring smile to Anij, then he followed the Son'a into the corridor. As they walked to the turbolift, the captain said, "It must have been strange for you."

Gallatin cast him a suspicious look. "What?"

"When you were a hostage," answered Picard.

"Being among the friends and families you knew so many years ago. All of them looking exactly as they did. Almost like . . . looking through the eyes of childhood again."

Gallatin stopped at the turbolift and pressed a panel to open the door. The captain kept talking, "And here you are, trying to *close* those eyes. You pretend you can't see what the bitterness has done to your people—what it's done to Ru'afo . . . and to you."

When the Son'a ignored him, Picard said, "It's turned you into a coward, a man who ignores his conscience."

The turbolift arrived, and Gallatin motioned with his weapon. "Get in."

Picard added, "A coward without the moral courage to stop an unspeakable atrocity. You *offend* me."

Gallatin stared at him. "Is this how a Federation officer begs for his life?"

"I'm not begging for my life, I'm begging for *yours*. There is still a way home, Gal'na."

Gallatin's face looked stretched with indecision. "Computer, close turbolift doors."

Once the doors were shut and they were alone, Gallatin lowered his weapon. "What you're asking me to do is . . . impossible."

"Do you know how to disable the injector?"

Gallatin nodded. "But I would need to be on the bridge. The crew is loyal to Ru'afo. An assault would fail."

"Perhaps we could lure him away," suggested Picard.

The Son'a shook his head. "It doesn't matter where he is. As soon as he realizes something is happening, he'll override my commands with one word to his comm link."

The captain frowned in thought, then smiled slyly. "What if he *doesn't* realize something's happening?"

Gallatin looked puzzledly at him, and Picard went on, "Can you get me to a transmitter? I have to speak with Worf and Data on the surface. We'll need their help."

With a scowl, Gallatin nodded. "Deck twelve," he told the computer.

On the bridge of the Son'a ship, Ru'afo watched his magnificent collector. Its huge sails extended into space, ready to suck the life-giving radiation out of the planet's rings. Ru'afo smiled to himself, looking forward to his moment of triumph. The Son'a would all be young again, and he would finally have his revenge after all these years.

What a fool I was to think the Federation would help me! No wonder those do-gooders had almost been defeated by everyone in the galaxy. He had offered them eternal youth, but they couldn't sacrifice a paltry six hundred people. It was their loss, and his gain.

"Initiate separation protocols," ordered Ru'afo. This was going to go very smoothly. First they had to activate and launch the injector assembly, to infuse the rings with a thermolytic charge. That would separate the metaphasic radiation, which the collector would pick up. What could be simpler?

A Tarlac officer worked his console. "Activating injector assembly."

"Separation in three minutes," reported an Elloran officer.

Ru'afo looked at his chronometer and watched with satisfaction as it ticked off the seconds. Suddenly the ship was jarred by an impact. He looked accusingly at his crew.

"A small craft is coming up from the surface," reported a Son'a officer. "It's firing tachyon bursts at us."

"On screen," ordered Ru'afo.

Cutting through the Briar Patch came a small, sleek craft. It was a Federation ship, he decided, probably the captain's yacht.

"One person aboard," said the Son'a officer. "It's the android."

"He's no threat," scoffed Ru'afo.

In the cockpit of the yacht, Data kept firing tachyon bursts at the huge Son'a ship. From his instruments, the android saw that the collector was almost at full power—they didn't have much time.

He pressed a comm panel and said, "Data to Picard."

"Yes, Data," came the captain's voice.

"Sir, they are ignoring my attack."

"Keep firing tachyon bursts into their shield grid," ordered Picard. "Is Worf in position?"

"Yes, sir. He is ready for simultaneous transport."

"We're approaching the bridge now. Picard out."

The android nodded grimly, then piloted the captain's yacht into a steep bank. Slowly he came around to unleash another stream of tachyon bursts.

On the bridge of the Son'a ship, an Elloran officer reported, "Separation in one minute."

The Son'a officer broke in, "Sir! The Federation ship is creating a disruption in our shields."

"If they go out of phase," said another crewman, "it will increase our exposure to the thermolytic reaction."

Ru'afo waved impatiently at them. "Very well. Destroy that ship and reset our shield harmonics. Do not delay the countdown."

The Son'a watched with satisfaction as their phaser fire pummeled the small ship. It wasn't destroyed, but it broke off its attack and veered toward the planet. *What a pitiful, last-ditch effort,* thought Ru'afo.

"The Federation ship has been disabled," reported a Tarlac officer.

"Separation in twenty seconds," said the Elloran on the science console.

Suddenly a flash of light blinded everyone on the

bridge. It only lasted a couple of seconds, but it was very disturbing.

"What is that?" demanded Ru'afo.

"I don't know," admitted another Son'a. "Systems don't seem to be affected."

"Separation in ten seconds," reported the Elloran officer.

Ru'afo looked with satisfaction at the countdown indicator. The huge sails unfolded from the collector, ready for action.

"Five seconds," reported an underling.

Ru'afo smiled as the thermolytic injector assembly was launched toward the planet. It set off a vast chain reaction in the rings of the planet. The rings changed colors, from a drab brown and yellow to a vibrant purple. Plumes of particulate matter swirled from the rings and scattered into space.

It's almost cleansing, thought Ru'afo. *Exactly as the simulations predicted—*

"Sir," broke in the Son'a officer, "I'm not showing any change in metaphasic flux levels."

Ru'afo strode to the man's station. "Your scanners must be malfunctioning."

The crewman stared in amazement at his console. "All ship functions are off-line!"

Ru'afo pushed him aside and began working the console himself. "How can there be no ship functions if the viewscreen is working? Artificial gravity is stable; life-support is stable."

Puzzled, the ahdar looked around the bridge, and something caught his eye. It was a small patch of black and yellow grid. He rushed toward the gap and carefully touched it to make sure his eyes weren't deceiving him. *No! It couldn't be!*

Ru'afo drew his phaser and fired it at the wall. The image faded away, revealing the hologrid underneath.

"It's a holodeck!" he shrieked as he fired again and again at different parts of the bridge. Every time he fired, another chunk of the bridge dissolved, until finally he found the staircase and the hatch.

Ru'afo climbed into the cockpit and found himself looking out the window at . . . *his own ship!* The planet's rings were normal, undamaged. Nothing had happened.

"We were transported to the holoship when we reset our shields," he told his crew. "Everything we saw . . . was an illusion."

Frantically, he pounded his comm link. "Ru'afo— authorization delta-two-one. Override all interlink commands to injector assembly one!"

"Unable to comply," replied the computer. "Injector assembly one has been deactivated."

Ru'afo threw his head back and roared in anger.

On the real Son'a bridge, Picard, Worf, and Gallatin were in command of all the consoles and ship's functions. The real countdown display showed twenty-seven seconds left, and it was frozen there.

Worf reported, "All injector subsystems are confirmed off-line."

Picard nodded. "Decloak the holoship and engage a tractor beam, Mr. Worf."

The holoship from the lake suddenly appeared on the viewscreen. Picard breathed a sigh of relief and pressed the comm panel. "Picard to Data."

He could hear tremendous static surrounding the android's voice. "Data here."

"Your status?"

"Precarious, sir. I am having trouble reentering the atmosphere—too much damage. I believe I will have to transport to the surface."

"Understood," answered Picard. "Well done."

"Thank you, sir."

Data transported out of the damaged yacht just as it entered the atmosphere. The yacht turned into a blazing fireball, then broke into a million glowing embers.

On the holoship, Ru'afo pounded his fist on the conn. He shouted at his crew, "This ship is equipped with fourteen long-range transporters. Are they *all* useless?"

A Tarlac reported, "They must have been locked and secured *after* we were beamed here."

"Isolate one," ordered Ru'afo, "and reroute its command sequence through the auxiliary processor."

With a pained expression, the officer looked at him. "Sir, there's nothing we can do. They already have control of our ship."

"I don't plan on going back to our ship," muttered Ru'afo.

On the Son'a bridge, Worf reported, "Captain, the *Enterprise* is within range."

"Let them know we're in command," ordered Picard.

Worf nodded and worked the unfamiliar console. "I'm putting Commander Riker through."

"Enterprise to Picard," came a familiar voice.

"Number one."

"We should be at your position in seven minutes," said Riker with relief in his voice. *"Do you need assistance?"*

"Negative. Did you succeed?"

"Yes. The Council has ordered a halt to the Ba'ku relocation while they conduct a top-level review."

"Top-level review?" Picard snorted. "There will be no cover-up of this. Not after I—"

"Captain!" Worf broke in. He motioned to the digital countdown display, which had reset to three minutes and was now ticking off again.

Gallatin saw the problem and began to work his instruments. Glumly, he shook his head. "The separation protocols have been reset on board the collector. I can't override."

"Scan for life signs," ordered Picard.

Worf plied his console. "One. It's Ru'afo."

"Can you beam him off?"

"Negative, sir. He's raised the shields."

The captain turned to Gallatin. "Is there any other way to disable the injector?"

The Son'a shook his head. "Not from here."

Captain Picard looked at the countdown display. It was 2:40 and falling—and there was nothing they could do to stop it.

CHAPTER
11

On the bridge of the Son'a ship, Gallatin furiously worked his console. Picard stepped toward him, with a glance at the countdown display. There were only two and a half minutes left before the thermolytic injector destroyed all life on the planet below. That included most of the Ba'ku, plus his comrades.

Ru'afo was alone on the collector, his shields up.

"If we could get into the collector," said Gallatin, "we could remove the ignition matrix directly from the injector assembly."

"Sir," Worf cut in, "there's a small opening in the shields at the base of the coupling adapter. I might be able to beam through it—" He highlighted the coupling and the injector on a schematic drawing.

"Remain at your post, Commander," ordered Picard, rushing toward the transporter pad.

As he pulled off his jacket, he glanced at Gallatin. "The ignition sequence—what can you tell me?"

"The thrusters activate one minute before separation. You'll see the cryogenic tanks venting. Don't use any laser tools or weapons after that—they could ignite the propellant exhaust. The substructure will retract fifteen seconds prior to separation."

Picard grabbed his phaser rifle and jumped on the transporter pad. "Energize!"

He materialized inside a cavernous chamber, full of spidery supports, pipes, and conduits. Recalling the schematic, Picard slung the rifle onto his back and began to climb toward the injector. This was not an area designed for manned operations, and he had to use the weblike supports and conduits to get from one narrow platform to another.

The captain paused near the base of one huge collector sail. He heard an alarm sounding in the distance, and he moved toward the sound. Suddenly a phaser beam hit the support, spattering him with molten metal. But Picard kept going.

Ru'afo fired several more shots, but the support beams afforded the captain some cover. He could see the injector assembly ahead of him—and Ru'afo was in the control booth. As Picard got closer, they stared into each other's eyes.

The Son'a rushed out of the booth and began to

descend toward the captain. Picard knew that he was looking to get a clear shot. With about a minute and a half left, there wasn't time for the captain to think about his own safety—he had to keep climbing.

Ru'afo stopped, took aim, and shot at the support where Picard was standing. It snapped in half, and the captain began to fall. He grabbed a pipe and swung himself through the spidery structure.

Letting go at the last second, Picard flew through the air and landed on a narrow plank. He instantly unslung his rifle and began to fire at Ru'afo, driving him back. He had him in his sights—one more shot would end it!

Suddenly the cryogenic tanks all around him began to vent nitrogen gas. *The pre-launch sequence had begun!* He could see the injector above him—ice was melting from it, as the beam fusion reactors powered on.

Now there's only a minute left, and I can't use my phaser. He climbed upward until he reached the injector, knowing that if he removed the ignition matrix, it would misfire. Picard found the access panel and had located the circuit board when he heard a voice:

"Stop!"

He turned to see Ru'afo moving toward him, his weapon leveled. Picard could see the countdown on the injector—it read forty-two seconds. Gas plumes spurted all around them, and both men looked sweaty and dirty.

"We're getting too old for this, Ru'afo," said Picard.

The Son'a snorted a laugh. "After today, that won't be a problem . . . for either of us."

"Separation in thirty seconds," said the computer on the injector.

Picard pointed to his weapon. "Are you really going to risk igniting the fumes?"

When Ru'afo didn't answer, Picard shrugged. "No? All right, then I will." He lifted his phaser rifle.

"No!"

Picard fired a single shot at the fumes, then dove into the booth for cover. The cavernous chamber was lit up by a tremendous explosion. Ru'afo was knocked backward by the impact, and his hood was thrown off. Picard stared at his stretched, stapled skin.

While Ru'afo was distracted, Picard reached into the access panel and grabbed the ignition matrix from the injector. Then he leaped onto a nearby platform. The injector was going to separate from the collector in a few seconds, and he didn't want to be on it!

In the smoke and haze, he saw Ru'afo climb onto the injector. The Son'a reached into the access panel, then looked up in horror.

Picard waved the circuit board at him. "Looking for this?"

With a loud clank, the support structure disengaged from the injector and began to pull back. Ru'afo's eyes filled with panic as he watched Picard move away from him. He took a step, afraid to jump.

The captain realized that Ru'afo would be launched

into space with the machine. He held out his hand and shouted, "Take my arm!"

The Son'a reached for him, but it was too late—they had moved too far apart. The captain watched helplessly as the countdown reached zero, and a forcefield enveloped the injector assembly. A moment later it shot into space.

He crawled to a viewscreen and watched the injector move into the planet's rings. The metaphasic dust and gases swirled all around it, like a colorful tornado. With the forcefield around the injector, it was possible that Ru'afo was still alive. *For how long?*

Picard didn't see the amazed Son'a as his face grew younger and younger. Just as he wanted. His body went back in time, from old man to young man . . . to teenager. Finally he was a boy, then a toddler, a baby . . . then he was just molecules.

Worf and Riker stood on the planet's surface, enjoying the homecoming of the Ba'ku to their lovely village. Friends and family laughed and hugged one another, while they told stories of their adventures.

Deanna Troi was on the hillside, walking with a group who had been captured. She waved to Riker, and he waved back.

Worf looked at his old comrade, thinking how natural it was for Will to be back with Deanna. Worf had once loved her, too; but with Deanna, every man walked in Will's shadow.

Riker caught Worf looking at him, and he smiled

sheepishly. "You think . . . when we get away from this place, it'll change the way we feel about each other?"

The Klingon shook his long, unruly hair. "Your feelings about her haven't changed since the day I met you, Commander. This place just let them out for a little fresh air."

Riker nodded. "Thanks. Better let the captain know that the *Ticonderoga* has moved into orbit."

"Yes, sir." Worf headed in the direction of the captain, who was talking with Anij and Sojef. As he walked, he passed Gallatin, standing at the edge of the fields. The Son'a, really an exiled Ba'ku, was watching the children play among the haystacks. He looked wistful and lost.

Worf joined the captain, Sojef, and Anij in the village. They were also watching Gallatin at the edge of the field.

"I wish there was some way to bring them back home," said Sojef.

"Ask them," said Picard.

"I'm afraid there's too much bitterness . . . on both sides."

Then they saw Dr. Crusher walking across the fields with a Ba'ku woman. They approached Gallatin and stopped to talk. They were too far away for Worf to hear what they said, but the woman studied Gallatin intently. Finally they embraced—as a mother embraces a long-lost son.

Anij looked at Picard. "Mother and son. You arranged this?"

Picard nodded. "I thought it might begin the healing process."

Sojef grinned and shook Picard's hand. His face showed his deep appreciation for everything this offlander had done for them. "Thank you."

Sojef ran off to join Gallatin and his mother.

"Captain," said Worf, "the *Ticonderoga* has moved into orbit." The Starfleet vessel would assume a position guarding the planet, while the Federation Council looked into the matter.

The other crew members moved off, and Picard found himself alone with Anij. This was a moment he knew had to come.

"What am I going to do without you?" asked Anij, her eyes begging him to stay.

"These are perilous times for the Federation," answered the captain. "I can't abandon it to people who would threaten everything I've spent a lifetime defending. I have to go back . . . if only to *slow things down* at the Federation Council."

Anij lowered her eyes, looking crushed.

Picard took her hand. "But I have three hundred and eighteen days of vacation coming. I plan on using them."

"I'll be here," answered Anij.

The captain took her in his arms, and they kissed.

Artim poked his head out of a haystack, then looked around for the other children. Beside him,

Data poked his head out of the hay and scanned the area as well.

"Data!" called a familiar voice. Artim knew it was Dr. Crusher. "It's time to go!"

"Let's hide," Artim told the android.

"I have to go now," said Data, jumping out of the haystack. "Bye."

"Bye," answered Artim. The boy jumped out of the haystack, too. He was sorry to see his new friend leave, but he had a feeling he would see him again. As they brushed the hay off their clothes, Artim's father joined them.

For the first time, Sojef looked at Data with fondness. "Mr. Data, I hope we will see you again."

The android nodded. Then he turned and strode toward his friends—Picard, Crusher, Troi, Riker, La Forge, and Worf.

Artim ran after him. "Hey, Data! Don't forget, you've got to play a little every day!"

"Good advice," agreed Riker.

"Enterprise," said Captain Picard, "seven to beam up."

In a flurry of sparkling lights, the offlanders disappeared from the planet of the Ba'ku. Artim knew he would miss them.

About the Author

John Vornholt has had several writing and performing careers, ranging from being a stuntman to writing animated children's cartoons, but he enjoys writing books most of all. He likes playing one-on-one with the readers. John has written over a dozen *Star Trek* books, plus novels set in such diverse universes as *Babylon 5* and *Sabrina, the Teenage Witch.* His fantasy novel about Aesop, *The Fabulist,* is being adapted as a musical for the stage.

John lives in Arizona with his wife, Nancy, and two kids, Sarah and Eric, and he goes roller-skating twice a week.

Send E-mail to John at: jbv@azstarnet.com